W9-CSH-129

CASINO

& OTHER STORIES

". . . beautifully written and shaped: a subtle substantial achievement."
— *Books in Canada*

"Readers who enjoyed *Women of Influence* (1989), Bonnie Burnard's first collection of stories, will, with her second, experience a jolt of familiar delight; in the powerful, quietly polished prose of *Casino and Other Stories* the old trademark tone — confident, a little wry — is honed to a fine-pointed edge."
— *Quill & Quire*

"Like Munro and Svendsen, Burnard demonstrates the continued vitality of the realist tradition in Canadian literature."
— *Toronto Star*

"*Casino* deserves to win prizes . . . These stories are resonantly detailed, with startling, even shocking twists . . ."
— *Globe and Mail*

CASINO

& OTHER STORIES

BONNIE BURNARD

A Phyllis Bruce Book
HarperPerennial
HarperCollins*PublishersLtd*

CASINO & OTHER STORIES. Copyright © 1994 by Bonnie Burnard.
All rights reserved. No part of this book may be used or
reproduced in any manner whatsoever without prior written
permission except in the case of brief quotations embodied in
reviews. For information address HarperCollins Publishers Ltd,
Suite 2900, 55 Avenue Road, Toronto, Canada M5R 3L2.

First published in hardcover by HarperCollins Publishers Ltd: 1994
First HarperPerennial edition: 1995

Canadian Cataloguing in Publication Data

Burnard, Bonnie
Casino & other stories

1st HarperPerennial ed.
"A Phyllis Bruce book".
ISBN 0-00-647961-8

I. Title.

PS8553.U65C3 1995   C813'.54   C94-932397-7
PR9199.3.B87C3 1995

98 99 ❖ HC 10 9 8 7 6 5 4 3 2

Printed and bound in the United States

For my brothers

CONTENTS

CASINO

& OTHER STORIES

CRUSH

It's Thursday morning and it's hot, hot, hot. The girl is painting the kitchen cupboards. The paint stinks up the room, stinks up the whole house. Her summer-blonde ponytail and her young brown shoulders are hidden in the cupboards, and a stranger coming into the kitchen, seeing only the rounded buttocks in the terrycloth shorts and the long well-formed legs, might think he was looking at part of a woman.

She's tired. She babysat last night. It's not the best job she can get; there are other kids, easier kids. She takes the job because of him, for the chance to ride alone with him in the dark on the way home. She thinks she's in love.

She remembers him at the beach, throwing his kids around in the water, teaching them not to be afraid. She doesn't try to imagine anything other than what she has seen, because it's already more than enough. His back and thighs she will remember when she is seventy and has forgotten others.

Her mother stands over the ironing board just inside the dining room door. Thunk, hiss, thunk, hiss. The kitchen table separates them. It has been piled impossibly high with dishes and cans of soup and corn and tea towels and bags of sugar and flour and pickling salt. Spice jars, pitched here and there, rest askew in the crevices of the pile. The cupboards are hot and empty. She has nearly finished painting them.

Neither the girl nor her mother has spoken for over an hour. It is too hot. She leans back out of the cupboards, unbuttons her blouse and takes it off, tossing it toward the table. It floats down over the dishes. She wants to take off her bra, but doesn't.

Her mother doesn't lift her head from the ironing. "You be careful Adam doesn't catch you in that state, young lady. He'll be coming through that door with the bread any minute." Her sleeveless housedress is stained with sweat. It soaks down toward her thick waist.

Maybe I want him to, the girl thinks.

"Have you picked out the bathing suit you want?" Her mother glances up at her. The bathing suit is to be the reward for the painting. "It's time you started to think about modesty. It's beginning to matter."

"No." The girl watches the fresh blue paint obliterate the

old pale green. She's lying. She has picked out her suit. It's the one on the dummy in the window downtown, the one the boys gather around. She knows she won't be allowed to have it. Mrs. Stewart in the ladies shop wouldn't even let her try it on, said it wasn't suitable for her. But it is. It's the one she wants.

She hears the scream of the ironing board as her mother folds it up and then she hears again her mother's voice.

"I'm going downtown for meat. You put that blouse on before I leave. Get it on. I'm as hot as you are and you don't see me throwing my clothes off."

Her mother stands checking the money in her billfold, waiting until the last button is secure before she moves toward the back door. "I'll bring you some cold pop." The screen door bangs.

The girl steps down from the paint-splattered chair. She goes to the sink and turns the water on full, letting it run to cold. She opens the freezer door, uses her thumbs to free the tray of ice-cubes. She fills a peanut butter glass with ice and slows the tap, watches the water cover the snapping cubes. She sips slowly, with her jaw locked, the ice bumps cold against her teeth as she drinks. She lifts a cube from the glass and holds it in her hand, feels it begin to soften against the heat of her palm. She raises her hand to her forehead and rubs the ice against her skin, back into her hair, down her cheek, down over her throat. The ice-cube is small now, just a round lump. Her hand is cold and wet.

His hand was wet when he danced with her at the Firemen's dance. Not the same wet though, not the same at all. His buddies stood around and hollered things about him liking the young stuff and everyone laughed, even the wives. She laughed too, pretending she understood how funny it was, his touching her. But she can still feel the pressure of his hand on her back, any time she wants to she can remember how it steadied her, how it moved her the way he wanted her to move. It should have been hard to move together, but it was easy, like dreaming.

She wonders how close he is to their house. She dries her hand on the tea towel hanging from the stove door. She undoes the top button of her blouse, then the next, and the next, and the next. It slips from her shoulders and lands in a heap on the floor. She unfastens her bra, eases it down over her brown arms, drops it.

She climbs back up on the chair and begins to paint again. Although the paint is thick and strong, she can't smell it any more. She works slowly, deliberately, the chair solid under her feet. The stale green paint disappears beneath the blue.

She turns at his sudden, humming entrance, the bang of the screen door no warning at all. He stands on the mat with the tray of fresh baking slung round his neck, shifting his weight from one foot to the other, suddenly quiet. She comes down from the chair, steps over the heap of her clothes and stands in front of him, as still as the surface of a hot summer lake.

"Jesus," he says.

"I wanted to show you," she says.

He backs out the door quickly, doesn't leave Thursday's two loaves of white and one whole wheat.

The girl can hear her mother's voice through the open back door. It sounds uneasy and unnaturally loud. She bends down and picks up her bra, although she knows there won't be time. She knows, too, that she will be punished, and in some new way.

He's in the truck and he's wishing he had farther to go than the next block. Lord, he thinks. What the hell was that?

He checks his rearview mirror. Her mother could come roaring out after him any minute. She could be forgiven for thinking there was something going on. He's a sitting duck in this damned truck. Just deliver your bread, he thinks. And then, Shit. A drive. He'll go for a drive. To clear his head.

He goes out past the gas station, past the beer store, out of the town onto a side road bordered by fence-high corn. He drives a few miles with the window down, letting the hot breeze pull the sweat from his face and arms. He eases the truck over to the shoulder.

He knows his only hope is that she tells her mother the truth. Which could be unlikely. Shit. If her mother decides he was in on it, there'll be phone calls, there'll be hell to pay. His wife won't believe it. He doesn't believe it and he was there.

Maybe the smart thing to do is just lie low and hope, pray, that her mother is embarrassed enough to keep her mouth shut. If it's going to come up, it'll come up soon and he'll just have to say it was a surprise, a real big surprise, and they can give him a lie detector on it if they want.

The girl has never given him even one small clue that she was thinking in those terms. And he can certainly see a clue coming. When he picks her up and drives her home, she always hides herself behind a pile of schoolbooks hunched up tight against her sweater. She's a good sitter, the kids love her. He likes talking to her and he always makes a point of being nice to her. And she helped him teach the kids to swim because his wife wouldn't, and he didn't even look at her, can't even picture her in a bathing suit.

So damned hot. He leans back in the seat, unbuttons his shirt and lights a Player's. The sight of her drifts back through the smoke that hangs around him. It's been a long time since he's seen fresh, smooth, hard breasts. Not centrefold stuff, not even as nice as his wife before the kids, but nice just the same. Yeah. Nice. He shifts around in his seat. Damn.

It's like she just discovered them. Or maybe she got tired of being the only one who knew. Now he knows and what the hell's he supposed to do about it? Man, this is too complicated for a Thursday morning.

The picture drifts back again and this time he holds it for a while. He's sure they've never been touched. He thinks about dancing with her that once and how easy she was in his arms. Not sexy, just easy. Like she trusted him. He can't remember ever feeling that before. They sure didn't trust him when he was seventeen, had no business trusting him. And what he gets from his wife isn't trust, not exactly.

She could be crazy. She's the age to be crazy. But he remembers her eyes on him and whatever it was they were saying, it had sweet all to do with crazy.

Back the picture comes again, and he closes his eyes and the breasts stay with him, safe behind the lids of his eyes. He can see a narrow waist, and squared shoulders. He hears words, just a few, although he doesn't know what they are, and he feels a gentleness come into his hands, he feels his cupped hands lift toward her skin and then he hears a racket near his feet and he opens his eyes to see a wretched crow on the open floor of the truck beside the bread tray; it's already clawed its way through the waxed paper, it's already buried its beak. He kicks hard and waves his arms and yells the bird away and he throws the truck in gear and tells himself out loud, "You're crazy, man, that's who's crazy."

The mother stands watching the girl do up the top button of her blouse. She holds the package of meat in one hand, the bottle of pop in the other. The pale brown paper around the meat is dark and soft where blood has seeped through. She walks over to the fridge, puts the meat in the meat keeper and the pop beside the quarts of milk on the top shelf. She closes the fridge door with the same care she would use on the bedroom door of a sleeping child. When she turns the girl has climbed up on the chair in front of the cupboards and is lifting the brush.

"Get down from that chair," she says.

The girl rests the brush across the top of the paint can and steps down.

"I could slap you," the mother says, calmly. This is not a conversation she has prepared herself for. This is not a conversation she ever expected to have. She cannot stop herself from looking at the girl's young body, cannot stop the memory of her own body and the sudden remorse she feels knowing it will never come back to her. She longs to feel the sting of a slap on her hand and to imagine the sting on the girl's cheek. But she pushes the anger aside, out of the way. She pulls a chair from the table, away from the mess of cupboard things piled there, and sits down in the middle of the room, unprotected.

"Sit down," she says.

The girl sits where she is, on the floor, her brown legs tucked under her bum as they were tucked through all the years of listening to fairy tales. The mother can smell her fear.

"How much did you take off?"

The girl does not answer. She looks directly into her mother's eyes and she does not answer.

The mother begins the only way she knows how.

"I had a crush on your father. That's how it started with us, because I had a crush on him. He was only a little older than me but I think it's the same. I don't know why it should happen with you so young, but I'm sure it's the same. The difference is I didn't take my clothes off for him. And he wasn't married. Do you understand? It's wrong to feel that way about someone if he's married and it's wrong to take your clothes off." She remembers other talks, remembers pulling the girl into her arms and carrying her up to bed.

The girl picks at a crusty scab on her ankle.

"The way you feel has got nothing to do with the way things are. You've embarrassed him. I could tell at the gate that he was embarrassed. You won't be babysitting for them any more. He'll tell his wife and they'll have a good laugh about it. You've made a fool of yourself." Oh, she thinks, don't say that.

"You will feel this way from now on. Off and on from now on. You have to learn to live with it. I wish it hadn't happened so soon. Now you just have to live with it longer. Do you understand?"

The girl shrugs her shoulders, lifts the scab from her skin.

"Women have this feeling so they will marry, so they will have children. It's like a grand plan. And you've got to learn to live within that plan. There will be a young man for you, it won't be long. Maybe five years. That's all. You've got to learn to control this thing, this feeling, until that young man is there for you."

The mother gets up from the chair and goes to the fridge. She takes out the pop and opens it, dividing it between two clean glasses which she takes from a tray on top of the fridge. She hands one to the girl, insisting.

"If you don't control it, you will waste it, bit by bit, and there won't be a young man, not to marry. And they'll take it from you, any of them, because they can't stop themselves from taking it. It's your responsibility not to offer it. You just have to wait, wait for the one young man and you be careful who he is, you think about it good and hard and then you marry him and then you offer it."

The girl gets up from the floor and puts her glass, still almost full, on the counter by the sink.

"I'd like to go now," she says.

The mother drains her glass. She feels barren. She is not a mother any more, not in the same way. It is as if the girl's undressing has wiped them both off the face of the earth.

The girl has run away from the house, out past the gas station and the beer store, onto a grid road that divides the corn-fields. She is sitting in a ditch, hidden, surrounded by long grass and thistles.

She knows she's ruined it, knows the babysitting days are over. Not because he was embarrassed. He wasn't embarrassed, he was afraid. It's the first time she's ever made anyone afraid.

She will find a way to tell him that she didn't mean to scare him.

She wishes her mother had just slapped her. She hears again the feelings her mother had about her father in some other time, some other century. She covers her ears. She hated having to hear it, it was awful, and that stuff about holding back and then getting married some day, she knows all about that. That's what all the women do, and it's likely what she'll end up doing because there doesn't seem to be any way to do anything else.

Except maybe once in a while. If she can learn not to scare people.

She feels absolutely alone and she likes it. She thinks about his back and his dark thighs and about standing there in the kitchen facing him. It's the best feeling she's ever had. She won't give it up.

She crosses her arms in front of her, puts one hand over each small breast and she knows she isn't wrong about this feeling. It is something she will trust, from now on. She leans back into the grass, throws her arms up over her head and stares, for as long as she can, at the hot July sun.

BREAKING THE LAW

At thirteen, Daniel often outsleeps his older sisters. Crystal thinks this is because he's growing. His body is day by day reproducing itself, expanding hard and fast: bones, muscles, skin, all of it. She assumes this growing takes place when he's at rest in his bed, with Pal asleep at his feet. Awake, he sometimes knocks things over with longer arms and larger hands that are an honest surprise to him, their force, their new distance from his body. Usually he sets things right again, books, cushions, coffee cups, asking without asking, Did I do that?

His sisters never sleep in. They are always up early, using the time before school to shower and to look into their respective mirrors, to fool with their hair and their faces, calling from the bathroom that they don't need breakfast while Crystal calls back that they are going to eat something. These exchanges usually waken Daniel. He dresses quickly, without the aid of a mirror, and bounds down the stairs to the kitchen. He sits at the breakfast bar with Crystal and eats eagerly, and then they share the *Globe and Mail.* He reads all of the sports stats and sometimes the news of the world and she reads around him until he's ready to leave for school.

By the time Daniel came down the stairs this morning, with the dog in tow, both of them hungry and still warm from sleep, his sisters had already left the house. He let Pal out the back door for a quick and necessary romp, fed him, and then got some cereal and sat down beside Crystal, close, so he could get at his share of the paper. Pal, who is part hound, part miscellaneous, emptied his dish quickly and followed, sliding in under the stool, rearranging himself until he could feel the comfortable weight of Daniel's feet on his back.

The big story in the Sports section was the sexual-assault charge against Mike Tyson; it had been given most of a page. Tyson's history, described in a grey sidebar for the reader's enlightenment, has been one of lawlessness and random violence.

Daniel snorted as he read. It wasn't a big surprise to him that Tyson is enormously wealthy and that the cars he's cracked up have been exotic. When Crystal asked, "What do you think about all this?" he offered only a young sports-lover's shrug, although as far as she knows what he loves is baseball. Then he muttered, "My hero," and went back to his stats.

On the television news the night before there had been

earnest discussion about the charge and its possible effect on Tyson's upcoming chance to regain the heavyweight title. They'd watched a boxing commentator, some jerk with a cigar and a sneer to accommodate it, bemoan the bad name the charge could give to boxing's honourable participants. It was an opportunity for Crystal to talk with Daniel about the innocent-until-proven-guilty benefits of living in a free country, but she'd let it pass.

Daniel stood up from his breakfast and then, as if to check something, he turned the paper back to the front page. Crystal had already read the news of the world with an earlier coffee, before Daniel came down. She'd already seen it. Gun control and broken cease-fires, distant massacres and well-funded wars, and in the midst of it all a one-column piece on another young man, this one pale and gaunt, who had been charged in a Milwaukee courtroom with sixteen counts of murder. She'd read the headline and then, unable to read the sentences in sequence, as the writer intended, her eyes had fallen chaotically down through the paragraphs to the end. She'd stopped at some of the worst of the words and then returned again to the beginning to reconfirm what she could not comprehend. The activity, carried out in some anonymous apartment, had gone unnoticed. His victims were young men, gay or black, or both. His car, if he had one, did not merit mention. And while Tyson proclaimed innocence, this man was quoted as

saying yes, I did that, and yes, that, too, he was willing, perhaps anxious, to tell exactly what he did, using ordinary
human verbs to describe his subhuman activity. He had taken
pictures, Polaroids, Crystal hoped; she refused to imagine
such pictures being developed anywhere. She assumed the pictures would help his prosecutors.

Crystal could see that Daniel was reading what she had
read, although he'd start at the beginning and move through
the piece as intended. "That's totally gross," he said, partway
through. "Puke city."

She told him that this man would either go to jail for a long
time or he'd go to a hospital for an indeterminate time.

Daniel said indeterminate means nobody knows how long,
right, and then he asked which did she think it should be? She
told him some of each, the hospital, but for a long time, for
eternity. He nodded, not necessarily in agreement but simply
to show that he understood what she was saying. Then he
asked, "What about Tyson?" Crystal told him if they could
prove he did it, she'd bet on two years in a really nice cell, with
a wide-screen TV and a fax machine and weights to lift and
maybe an extra bunk set up for his trainer, because Tyson's
people couldn't afford to let all that educated power just sit
there and rot. For this she got a look. While Daniel may be
impressed with the potential of his own disdain, he doesn't like
it if Crystal succumbs. He expects better.

She gathered the breakfast dishes and carried them over to the sink, watched the hot water fill the bowls. Daniel left to do his teeth and hair and then came back because he'd forgotten to get his lunch out of the fridge. He wandered around the kitchen, checked his watch, opened the fridge again to take a slug of orange juice from the bottle. He folded the *Globe and Mail* and dropped it on the pile for recycling in the corner by the phone, grabbed his satchel and then leaned over to talk to Pal, who long ago mastered the skill of following his every move without tripping him. When he walked by for the last time, he threw his arm heavily over Crystal's shoulder and then around her neck in a cumbersome hug, half affection, half attack.

And now he's gone, his young head crammed with sports stats and an ordinary Tuesday morning's news. Pal is curled up on his mat by the back door, although he's not dumb enough to sit there all day. He'll come to her soon, ready to make do until his life picks up again.

Crystal pours a coffee and lifts the *Globe* from the top of the recycling pile. She sits at the counter again and turns to the comics to see if Pogo has any wisdom to offer this morning, but she is thinking about Daniel. He will be cruising down the back lane on his way to school, likely snarling at some of the neighbourhood cats as they do their garbage rounds, veering toward them with his bike. She has asked him to stop and he said okay, but she doesn't know if he has, he might still be doing it on the sly. He says he does this for Pal, who cannot, according to a city by-law, join the cats on the outside unless he's on a leash. His sisters report that Daniel "emits noxious fumes" loudly and deliberately whenever Crystal is out of the house, just to make them crazy. She gives him some slack, tells them she'd bet the mortgage that many a decent man has, in his misspent youth, farted for fun. When she tells this, Daniel laughs a little secret laugh and the girls hoot in disgusted disbelief. She knows he taunts his sisters, sometimes with cracks about their make-up or about their friends, who could soon be his friends if he'd just watch himself, sometimes with lurid descriptions of his immi- nent armpit hair, telling them that he'll never ever have to shave it, ha, ha, ha, ha. Usually they just groan him out, but she won- ders if this could be a mistake; he's starting to play to the groans. A couple of times, when she was tired, or in the middle of some- thing, she laughed at him, mocked him, cruelly. She has had to remind herself that some of this behaviour should be attributed to the hormone soup sloshing through his new body. She is confident of eventual improvement, hints of which are evident if you know where to look, how to listen, what to listen for.

Pal nudges her bare foot with his damp nose. He needs to go outside again. He's been doing this more and more lately. Unable to relieve himself fully the first time, he has to ask to go again. He's old. "Okay, boy," she says. She quickly gets another coffee and takes him out the back door. Pal has always been Daniel's dog. Once, when Daniel was only three or four, a visiting playmate had smashed his favourite old truck to smithereens with a sturdy little toy hammer and Daniel had stood up and kicked the other child. When Crystal pulled him by the arm to separate him from the other boy, he yelled a loud surprising yell, and Pal arrived from nowhere, skidding on the hardwood floor as he took the corner. He barked once and made his decision, taking her ankle firmly in his jaws. And he meant business. It wasn't play. Her husband, who was still with them then, heard her call his name and came running into the room and grabbed Pal, carried him yelping to the garage to discipline him somehow, and that was the last real bite, but the loyalty was set.

She sits down on the edge of the deck and leans back to look up at the sky while Pal sniffs and rolls and romps arthritically around his yard. There are no clouds at all, it's a wide open prairie blue. The birds in the elms are loud, well fed. Pal stretches out in his usual far corner of the grass under the sun, calmly watching the sparrows fly from one elm to another, giving restrained attention to the cats as they roam the lane on the free side of the fence, occasionally checking on her. When he gets up and walks toward her she can see that the list he's developed is getting worse. He means to walk straight to her but he can't do it; he has to fight his own corrupted muscles just to cross the yard. He's come for a quick bit of assurance that he's still a real dog, and she takes his silky ears in both hands and scratches hard, saying yes, yes, yes, and oh, he's a good dog, he's a fine dog, our Pal. He growls his odd, contented growl and Crystal nods at him as if he's said something she can agree with, and then, as she watches him struggle back across the grass to his corner of the universe, she thinks, for the first time in maybe twenty years, about the dogfights.

One of the three blacktops leaving her town was only eight miles long. When you came to the stop sign at the end of it, you either had to turn around and drive back home or turn onto the main highway that led west to the States or east to London and Toronto. People called the road the Eight Mile. When strangers who had cut over to take a drive along the shore of Lake Huron somehow got themselves turned around and had to stop in the town to ask for directions, slowing their cars, leaning out their open windows, they were told, sincerely, just take the Eight Mile, uptown at the stop sign.

At the junction where the Eight Mile met the big highway there was a truck stop and, set back a few hundred yards beside a cornfield, an old barn. Most of the barns along the road had been repaired and painted bright red by the Dutch farmers who were moving in and buying up farmland, but the Eight Mile barn had never been painted and it wasn't used to house implements or livestock or crops. It was used for dogfights.

The owner of the truck stop had installed big floodlights to guide the semis in, and if you were driving out there late at night you could see the trucks from miles back, parked in front or pulling in or out onto the highway. Sometimes, if you looked off to the left a little, just beyond the dome of light around the truck stop, you could see the dark shapes of cars and pick-ups parked back near the barn.

The truck stop did a good business. It was renowned far and wide for its hot beef sandwiches and for the fresh pies prepared by stocky women who held that food should be good, should be a reflection on themselves, who religiously and suspiciously inspected pork and fish and corn and bananas and cream for taints or bruises or what they called uninvited livestock.

Sometimes, to keep the night going, Crystal and her friends would drive out to the truck stop after a Saturday night dance at the arena. They would sit in a booth near the back and share hamburgers or cream pie and smoke a few illicit cigarettes, and each of them would tell the others exactly what kind of night she'd really had. The truckers who had pulled in for gas and oil and pie and strong black coffee, men from distant places, took notice of the girls if they were on their own. They would grin and banter back and forth among themselves, their comments quick and quiet, cracks about lipstick or crinolines or spike heels, which the girls pretended to ignore but accepted wholeheartedly as either flattery or ridicule, depending on the wildly fluctuating state of their self-confidence. If some of the guys from the dance had decided to follow them out to the truck stop, if the dance had turned into an extended party, the truckers didn't say as much. Sometimes they'd nod toward the booth but there was no bantering. It was as if they'd seen different girls the last time.

She doesn't remember how she first learned about the fights in the barn and the betting, or from whom. Perhaps it was from her father, who must have known about them, although not firsthand. You had to know someone who knew someone and it's not likely that her father did. He was a local businessman, a conservative Christian capitalist. He would not have been welcome at a dogfight.

Although he did break the law sometimes. Whenever Carl Bressette came in from the reserve to sell his illegal fish at their back door, the law was broken. Her mother would open the screen door so Carl could step in, she was a firm believer in seasonal food and she wanted the fish all right, it was the best whitefish available anywhere, but she wouldn't take part in the transaction. She'd call Crystal's father to do it. Carl would talk to her father for a bit about the weather, they'd use brief phrases like, not a bad day, or, that was some storm Tuesday, and then he'd say, I've got some whitefish here for you, John, caught this morning, and he'd hand over a long cool package wrapped in newspaper, secured with twine. Her father would say, Thank you, thank you for remembering us, and Carl would zip up his jacket again and say, No trouble, and then he'd open the screen door as if to go, as if the exchange was finished. But he'd turn back just as her father was pulling his billfold from his back pocket and say, Could you by any chance lend me five bucks, John? I'm a little short. And her father would answer, Yes, I can spare five dollars, Carl. And finally, wanting to stay on Carl's shortlist, he would repeat, I appreciate your remembering us.

Perhaps she'd learned about the dogfights from recess talk on the dusty playground. In the noisy expanse between the school's narrow back doors and the distant eight-foot playground fence, exotic chunks of information, at once random and relevant, were often exchanged by young minds bored with the countries of South America, the invention of penicillin. Although how much of this information was reliable and how much sheer invention, gruesome new stories created only to showcase gruesome but treasured words like *pus* and *screamed* and *guts*, was anyone's guess.

Certainly no one she knew talked about taking a drive out the Eight Mile to maybe make a bit of money on the dogs. The fights were not advertised in the weekly paper. There were no announcements stapled to the telephone poles uptown. Crystal could have spent a lot of time trying to get someone to talk about those evenings in the barn but she knew even then she wouldn't have learned much. The OPP might have known about the fights and about the betting, but she didn't ever hear about any raids. It could have been seen as just a bit of quiet fun.

She remembers an after-supper drive out the Eight Mile in a brand-new bottle green Buick, the youngest of her older brothers intent at the wheel, pushing it, seeing what it would do. He hadn't invited her, she'd simply said she'd like to go when he asked their father for the keys, making herself part of the deal. Her presence in the car was intended to slow him down but it didn't, and she didn't want it to. It was late fall and she can remember the just harvested cornfields and the low wire fences flying by and the night air coming in through the open power windows, her hair wild in the wind, her face cold. She can remember the darkness inside and out and the yellow iridescence from the circle gauges on the dash. She had an oblivious confidence in the bottle green Buick and in her brother, more perhaps, she thinks now, than he had in himself. It didn't occur to her that their behaviour was dangerously stupid. She measured nothing, judged little.

When they got to the end of the Eight Mile her brother said they might as well grab a Coke, and he pulled into the truck stop lot and parked the new Buick beside a hulking semi. Walking in, she noticed activity over at the barn and she nudged him to look, asked if he knew about the fights. He just shrugged and said, "Doesn't everybody?" When she pushed him for details, about the dogs, about the men, he looked down at her with an impatience she was quite used to and asked how in hell would he know.

She never dreamed of getting into the barn, although it might have been possible, she'd got into lots of other places where she had no business. And she never tried to imagine what the dogs might look like fighting, or to put faces on the men standing around the ring watching. All she knew was that sometimes there were dogfights and betting in the barn at the end of the Eight Mile. You could call it a childhood mystery.

Now, in middle age, she finds it possible to imagine the fights, although they can only be imagined, she has neither sought nor gained any accurate information. She just makes the details up, pulls them from the air. She's never been in an empty barn, but the picture she gets is of moonlight seeping in through cracks and knotholes in the weathered walls, sturdy grey posts supporting heavy cross beams and maybe some frayed rope left behind on the cement floor, maybe a shovel or two. Any sound would be intermittent, from mice and swallows, or bats floating in the shadows under the high-pitched roof.

When the fights were on, there would have been a ring squared off somehow in the middle of the floor. There would have been a kerosene lantern or two, and they might have laid a few planks across some empty wood crates to serve as makeshift bleachers. And there was likely a central table of sorts for the rye and the Coke and the cups so the bettors could help themselves as they paid each other off. Initially, the dogs would be kept separate, in different corners of the barn, their leashes firmly gripped by those who had trained them, their excitement held in check until they could be set free.

When she closes in on two dogs going at it in the ring, she can see a white dog and a dark dog, not obviously matched in size or age or strength. As the dogs move, the light thrown by the lanterns is filled with their moving shadows. The cement floor is wet and slippery, maybe permanently stained. And the noise is monstrous. The white dog is very clean, he is small and afraid but smart and quick, tenacious, his eyes remain locked on the larger dog's throat. Where the white dog leaps, the dark dog broods, moves with more deliberation, and more force. In the dim light, the blood soaking through his thick dark coat has an almost purple sheen.

She wonders how the dogs were destroyed, the ones that lost. Likely just a trip out the side door with a burlap bag and a shotgun, maybe by the end of the night some truck bed was half full of blood-soaked burlap bags. But she thinks the dogs could have healed with time and might have fought again. Surely losing would give a dog an edge, make him a more deadly fighter. A better bet.

Still looking into the broad blue prairie sky, Crystal laughs aloud, the sound low and private, blunted. She has cast the dogs as David and Goliath, underdog and top dog. She has enriched the colours, directed the movement, dramatized the light, heard specific sounds which were not necessarily heard by anyone in attendance. She has imposed the grid of good and evil, invoked the most simpleminded of metaphors when she knows full well they were only terrified dogs, trained to rip into each other for the pleasure of those who cheered them on. She has almost obliterated the real words: *foul, familiar, barbaric,* not at all unique to the Eight Mile barn. She wonders why this is so natural to do, so irresistible.

She knows this morning's news isn't really news to Daniel: a one-time champion up for sexual assault, a decapitated head waiting in a fridge. He could tell you other things. He's got at his fingertips all the hideous specifics she once thought she wanted and couldn't quite get her hands on, all those and more, the barns thrown open now, the lights on full. There is no distance to travel, no darkness to see through.

She wants to call the *Globe and Mail*, collect, ask to talk to an editor. She thinks she could try to make it clear to him that she is sane. She could try to make it clear to him that she is not over some edge, that all she wants to do is convince him that he should make room in the midst of his other news, one page would seem generous, for a full-colour Saturday spread on Daniel's Ontario uncles, who are nothing more than grown-up, dependable, funny, complicated, sorrowful, good men. Grown-up, dependable, funny, complicated, sorrowful, good men who don't lay money on bleeding dogs in dark barns, or pound other men's skulls, or dream in madness.

He could use that picture of them sitting on the side deck in their cottage T-shirts listening to the Jays game, stretching their winter-white legs in the sun, wearing their stupidest hats to save the pink flesh on their skulls from exposure. It's a good clear shot. It would reproduce.

She thinks she could find and enlarge and frame the picture of Daniel on his absent father's knee, when he was just weeks old. In the picture you can see the newspaper thrown down beside them on the couch, you can see one large hand cupping Daniel's chin, supporting his head as they both wait patiently for the burp, their faces calm and hopeful. The other hand, hidden from the camera, rubs his small back with a steady, measured force which, somewhere in his bones, he should remember.

CASINO

THE CASINO was built back from the beach, up in the dunes overlooking the lake. You can see it for miles. It's a solid, bulky two-storey building, they paint it creamy yellow every couple of years, and it's always had a dark red roof.

Inside there is a long counter where you line up to buy ice cream and Popsicles and cold drinks and nickel bags of chips, and beyond the counter there is a row of slot machines, and two carousels of postcards, mostly pictures of Mounties or giddy long-legged women in short shorts and pigtails. The public washrooms, off in the corner, aren't all that clean. The floor is just cement because people bring sand in on their feet and lake water drips from their bathing suits, leaving small puddles.

Six wood pillars support the dance floor upstairs and when there's a dance on you can stand underneath, near a slot machine for instance, and imagine that the whole thing is going to cave in on you.

On a Saturday night, the dancers park bumper to bumper on the hard sand beside the Casino, maybe lean against their cars for a few minutes to take in some lake air or talk to someone they haven't seen in a while, and then they walk in through the big double doors, which are always wide open. Just inside the doors they pay their fifty cents and get the back of their hands stamped, sometimes with a flag, sometimes with a small blue rose, and then they turn left up the worn oak staircase. The staircase was once a classic, it was built double wide, wide enough for three or four to walk abreast and with easy shallow risers, but it's taken quite a bit of damage from the years of use and from the wet air off the lake.

Upstairs, on the far side of the room, there is a large stage recessed into the wall, about three feet off the floor, and tucked behind the stage, accessible only by a steep back staircase, four small rooms hold narrow beds for the university students who work the long counter downstairs. But most of the upstairs is nothing but open dance floor, a proper dance floor, hardwood of some kind, likely the most costly part of the entire building. And, although the span on this second floor is significant, there are no support pillars to spoil the movement of the dancers. That cost something too.

There is a balcony surrounding the dance floor on all but the bandstand side. It must be ten feet wide. You can dance out there if you want some privacy, and when a couple leaves the dance floor and goes out to the balcony they are pretty much left alone. If a storm comes up on a Saturday night there are hinged shutters which can be dropped to enclose the balcony, to make a box, and when this happens there are lots of people who know how to do it. Anyone can help. Through the week, the shutters are closed, but when the Saturday night dance is on, the view is magnificent.

There are no tables surrounding the dance floor, no chairs. Liquor is not served. On a Saturday night, any booze at the dance is already at work in somebody's bloodstream, although some of the older men will sometimes pack a hip flask. The police take turns dropping in and they stand around for a while with their arms folded, leaning against the wall opposite the bandstand, talking to people. They live in town in rented houses, play ball with some of the men. They gauge the level of drunkenness in the crowd and they are expected to do this. They get paid to know where trouble is likely to start. But the young men seem to know when the cops are coming, they are able to watch and read a pattern. They make lots of trips out to the parking lot to get their bottles from under the seats of their cars.

On most Saturday nights, the floor is packed tight with couples moving to the music. The music pours out through the open balcony and waves of moist air come in off the lake to refresh the dancers.

THE BEACH is wide, composed of fine white sand. At least it looks white, especially at night. But the individual grains are really tan, interspersed with black. It's always a surprise to find black grains, but you can see them in the daytime when you take a handful of sand and let it sift through your fingers. Black like pepper. Tall beach grass grows in the dunes around the Casino, but not down on the beach itself. There, the sand is bare and flat. The placement of the Casino, up in the drifting dunes, is a precaution against the occasional year when Lake Huron wants more of the beach for itself. This does happen. A few times, loud, pounding waves have come very close to the foundation and sometimes a wild summer storm will leave dark and surprisingly large pieces of driftwood high up in the dunes. But usually the lake throws only small casual waves and always the depth of the water increases very gradually.

You can teach children to swim at this beach. There are no sudden drops to frighten them, no rocks, no mysterious under-growth. There is nothing on the bottom but small parallel waves of sand, which can be seen clearly through the water. Minnows abound, but children are not afraid of minnows. And if you swim out far enough, just beyond shoulder depth if you are ten or eleven, you are rewarded with a sandbar. Suddenly you can stand up and shout to the shore and the water is only at your waist. Then you can swim back, toward the Casino. There are more sandbars, of course, farther out, but you don't get to stand up on them; they're just there, beneath you. Children who are brought to this beach can often do a handstand in the water before they can swim in it. And swimming with your eyes wide open is a piece of cake.

The Casino road is a sticky blacktop, it cools faster than the white hot afternoon sand. There are a dozen buildings along this road. There is a new drive-in where teenaged girls in short shorts and crisp sleeveless summer blouses carry trays of burgers and shakes to cars full of tired families or wide-awake young men. There is a roller rink and a mini-golf and a deserted cement-block hotel, left over from another era. Behind the hotel there is a small permanently locked ice-house. Older cottagers can remember the snakes that disappeared in all directions when you pulled a block of ice from the sawdust which kept it hard in the summer heat. And behind all these commercial establishments are the cottages, the originals, with screened porches and substantial stone fireplaces and good dry wood stacked somewhere near the back door. Most of the cottages have weathered nameplates nailed above their front screen doors: Thistle Do Me, Dunworkin, Tipperary, Lakeview.

On summer Saturday nights, the sun moves down over the lake just as the dance is getting under way. That's when the air cools. The water and the sky above it absorb the colours left behind by the sun and older people who are not at the dance sit in their screened porches or walk the beach just to see these colours. Later, the lake goes dark and the light from the moon and the stars shows silver on the waves. Sometimes the entire face of the lake is silver.

You can see this from the Casino balcony, when you're not dancing.

THE BAND is always the same. It is composed of five men, only one of whom is over twenty-five, and he's way over. There are two guitars, a fiddle, drums and a piano. The older man plays either the piano or the fiddle, switching off with the young man who might be his son. The lead singer plays guitar and is very good looking. He is cute, to use the vernacular. The crushes on him almost bounce off the walls. But he's learned how to flash a quick smile without engaging in what could be construed as meaningful eye contact. He has a young wife and sometimes she comes to the dances, but not always.

The band members don't wear jeans or jackets or string ties. They're dressed in khaki pants and nice short-sleeved summer shirts. Their repertoire suits the crowd just fine. Some jives early on, slow songs for slow dancing a little later, then, to bring everyone back to the sweaty earth, a polka or two, and a square dance if the older man who plays the fiddle and the piano sees enough dancers in the crowd to get it going properly. He calls the squares and he is not much amused by the young types who assume positions and then bugger it up for everyone, mocking each formation as he calls it. Near the end of the evening the band plays "Send Me the Pillow That You Dream On" and they always close with Patsy Cline's "Sweet Dreams." If you haven't got your arms around someone good by "Send Me the Pillow," there's hardly any time left, "Sweet Dreams" is coming fast.

The guys in the band must watch the couplings and the quarrels, but they don't show much interest. They are discreet, at least while they play. Maybe later they talk about the dancers, and the non-dancers; maybe they have cruel things saved up to say to each other, or funny things. Maybe they see the dance as a show to watch, just something to enjoy.

DUNCAN is seventeen and blond and vain, although he would say he's just confident. On most Saturday nights, second only to the lead singer in the band, he's the cutest guy at the dance and he knows it. He looks a bit like Ricky Nelson, even his sister tells him this, but he carries himself like James Dean. He loves movies. He's got the confused sulk down pretty good and he knows when to smile, how to make it spread out around him. He gets by in school. His teachers in the small high school in the town just eight miles inland are agreed that he's a lot brighter than he pretends to be, and they're all passing him, with B's, and a few C's to show they mean business. They're waiting for him to click into gear, to stop being James Dean and start being whatever it is he can be. He dresses for the dances in tan pants and a lightweight pastel V-neck sweater, both pressed by his mother, he won't wear anything wrinkled, and in white bucks which he saved for and drove alone across the Bluewater Bridge to Port Huron to buy. The white bucks are usually impeccable.

He's got a friend, Jack, and they hang out together, loosely. Sometimes they get a bottle of rye to keep in the car, sometimes they don't bother. The police don't pay much attention to them.

On a typical Saturday night, Duncan dances twice, maybe three times. Although his sister is usually at the dance with her friends, he wouldn't touch her with a ten-foot pole. If she asks him for money, he'll give her some, but he doesn't want to get involved in her little world. She's got one friend, Donna, who hangs around the house a lot. Donna's pretty good, she just naturally sees the bright side of things and she can be relied upon to help him with his algebra, so he usually dances with her, one song only. Soon after he takes her back to the wall someone else will approach her, and Duncan understands that his dancing with her gets her started for the night. He figures it's the least he can do. Once, while he was guiding her around the floor, Donna told him a dirty joke, she whispered it into his ear. He was pretty disgusted.

He waits awhile before he dances again, leaning against the wall, talking to Jack or some of the other guys, sometimes to one of the cops. Usually there are American girls at the dance, lots of Americans own cottages. He always waits and watches and picks out the best one. They're different from his sister and Donna and the others. Their clothes are always one year better. And they draw attention to themselves on purpose, laughing, flirting, coming up the stairs sometimes alone, like they don't care. Duncan thinks maybe they don't care and this frightens and impresses him. He doesn't really know any of them, except their names, everyone knows their names.

When he gets his arms around one of them, she'll settle right down, she'll become quiet and talk to him and ask him questions, softly. Just the opposite of the girls from town. They're like scared birds until you ask them to dance, and then they get stupid, silly, loud in your arms.

He likes to save the last dance for the lead singer's wife, if she's there. She's the only woman he knows who smells the same all the time, some perfume she wears. He's not nearly the dancer she is but he doesn't mind, he lets her lead him around the floor. When they're dancing she sometimes waves to the band, he can feel her hand lift from his shoulder and he knows she's smiling. Once, when they were as far away from the band as you can get, he tried to pull her a little closer, but her arms turned into steel, holding him where he was.

DUNCAN will survive his James Dean phase. Donna will pound enough algebra into his head to ensure his acceptance to a good university, which his parents will pay for, as they planned all along. He will study law, having determined at the ripe old age of twenty that what people are best at is getting themselves into trouble, and that there's a dependable and generous living to be made from this inevitability. He won't marry Donna. He won't marry anyone until he's finished his law degree. This first wife will be pale and willowy, until about the third child. By the time the fifth is born, she won't look anything like the woman he married and he'll trade up to a dark academic who looks at thirty-eight pretty much the way she'll look for the rest of her life. Eventually, at a Christmas dinner with parents and wives and husbands and kids, after a bad year all round, including some tricky business with prostate cancer, his sister will call him a little snob. He will calmly respond that he will never cease to be amused by her intensity. She will dig in then, remind him of mediocre marks and of Donna, who will have had a hysterectomy at twenty-three and married no one. In mid-life, he will attend only an occasional dance at his golf club and take the proffered hand of his second wife, reluctantly.

JACK is skinny, really skinny. And tall. He towers over Duncan. His mother has a terrible time finding pants to fit him. He considers his physical state to be temporary, and he largely ignores his clothes and any talk about them, or about his body. He is happiest when he forgets himself entirely. He has a game going where he can get through a whole evening as if he has no physical presence at all, as if he's invisible. He can have a great time this way. He's not as smart as Duncan but he pulls down better marks; he's what the teachers call a worker. He doesn't mind schoolwork. It's just like anything else, a garage to clean out, a yard to mow, you do it, check it over, make damn sure you don't have to do it twice.

He goes to the dances all the time, usually rides out with Duncan. He'll beg a bottle from his older brother if Duncan wants one, and when he drinks he gets pretty loose pretty fast but all this does is make the laughs come easier. Everyone thinks he's funny, and he is. He's good company. The cops know him and they watch to make sure he doesn't get behind the wheel when the dance is over, other than that they leave him alone.

He dances a lot. He'll dance with anyone. Girls will walk up and grab him when they need a partner. Even for slow dances. They give him little bits of stuff, a touch here, a breast against a forearm there. This just makes him happy. It would never occur to him to make a move on one of them; he's waiting until his body is better developed, until it's something a girl might want. He believes in the future.

He figures the American girls are from outer space. But after they catch on that he can be asked to dance, they won't be stopped. So he dances. When they ask him about his family or his school or his summer job, he lies through his teeth, tells them he's rich and brilliant, a superachiever. He told one girl he had six offers of a summer job. And she said exactly what he wanted her to say. That's wonderful. None of the ones from town ever say that, not to him, anyway. If the girls forget themselves and cuddle into him during a slow dance, he can make his body disappear altogether. They can't get at him.

He's got magazines at home, hidden between his mattress and his box spring, and when he wants to imagine what the future will be like, when he's heavier and not so clumsy, he pulls them out. He gets the magazines from his brother's stash, takes two or three at a time and trades them around. If he got caught, he'd get killed, but his brother isn't all that organized.

Jack is the one who told Donna the dirty joke. When Duncan tells it back to him in the car on the way home, he just laughs all over again.

JACK will run into trouble in university. He will get tired of having to work harder than the other guys. He will meet his residence roommate's cousin right before Christmas in his first year and start to date her, seriously. He will listen to her, he'll hear all kinds of things he never dreamed of. She will invite him to touch her and claim that she loves his long body and he'll fall, hook, line and sinker. He'll quit school and move around a bit from one joe job to another, trying to avoid the accusations in his parents' eyes. And then he'll take her home to meet them and they'll see that for the first time he's not laughing, he's just terribly happy. His mother will lie beside his father in their bed and whisper, this girl loves him, this is his chance.

He will get a job as the manager of an arena in a town not far away from his own and father four children, three of whom will go to university, and prosper. One of his sons will run into trouble in his teens. There will be bad marks and senseless theft and drugs and kitchen fights and lots of appointments with well-dressed counsellors in the city. Eventually the kid will come round, more or less. His wife will have one embarrassing mid-life affair, an intense ridiculous passion, which she will take with her to the grave. Jack will remain extraordinarily thin all his life, as will his sons. When he is quite old, he will remember the Casino and the Saturday-night dances. He will remember the words of songs and the way the lake smelled different after dark. But he won't be able to remember which of the Rawlings boys was his friend those summers. His wife won't know, of course. She wasn't there.

GRADY is quite a bit older than the others at the dances, grey hair and less of it, bad veins in his legs, a paunch, some shrapnel. He still wears his hair cropped short, army style, and he usually has a cigarette tucked behind his right ear, although he hasn't touched tobacco for years, not since his chest started to tighten up on him.

He's married all right but he doesn't ask his wife to come to the dances any more. She's been born again and she's changed, changed in every way. Grady tells people that he's hoping she can get herself born just one more time. He spends most evenings out of the house, his own house, bought and paid for, and he can't even relax in it. Sometimes he tries but she hovers around him for no reason, breathing over his shoulder if he's reading something, changing the channel on him if he's watching TV. Often he'll walk uptown to the poolroom, which is respectfully called the library by most of its patrons. The talk's pretty good there and there's usually an opportunity to lighten the pockets of some of the apprentices by a few bucks. Grady's wife has given up trying to convert him, now she just notes his sins. She's got a list, he's sure, hidden away somewhere with her other religious stuff. She never was what you'd call a party girl but she could dance, she could at least dance.

Grady works whenever he can, picking up a few months at the canning factory, a few months with the town. And he makes himself generally available for odd jobs; people stop him on the street and ask if he's got some time, if he could do a job, and he always says, Just name it. He knows damn near every shingle in the town like the back of his hand and he's poured more than his share of cement. He gets a bit of a pension cheque from the war. He was old to go but he went anyway. He figured he wasn't exactly vital to the home front and he was fit. He didn't like to see the young guys taking it all on. When it was over, they put him in the vets hospital and opened his hip to go after the shrapnel he'd brought home with him from France but there's some there still, he can feel it from the inside if he moves the wrong way.

He goes to the dances to watch and to lean against the wall and talk, find out what's going on. He likes to talk to the cops. He's not at all troubled by a uniform. Sometimes he'll watch and quietly point out a stumble or a stagger, he knows without even thinking which of the pups is the most likely to overdo it. He collects most of his cigarettes leaning against the wall at the Casino. When there's a lull in the conversation someone usually offers a pack of smokes around and he always takes one, to be polite, and tucks it behind his ear, where it stays until it falls out later, broken, on his pillow.

He'd never bother the young girls with his attentions, although he does love to watch them move, he does love the summer colours of their sundresses and their brown arms and their white sandals. Whenever Grady catches himself starting to think about sex, he pulls up short. Only if there's a polka or a square dance and he can see that he's needed will he let someone drag him onto the floor. He pays the price for days after, the price being short hard pains like shards of glass drifting around loose in his blood, but what the hell, he figures, life's for fun, ain't it?

He thinks the American kids are a huge pain in the ass. He hates to see the girls from town batting their eyelashes at the suntanned boys from the U.S. of A. And he could throttle the pups who prance around trying to catch the attention of the half-dressed girls from over the border when there are so many of their own to choose from. Grady has always thought the Americans were a little late to the war.

He was the one who told Jack the joke in the first place, the one Jack told to Donna, who told it to Duncan, who was disgusted. If Grady knew that Duncan was disgusted by something as ordinary as a little off-colour joke, he'd call him a candy ass. He'd take him out for a walk around the balcony and tell him a couple of stories from France that would straighten his curlies. Disgusted? What a goddamned pup.

GRADY will outlive his good wife by quite a few years. He will help her when she is dying, bringing tea and arrowroot biscuits to the bed on a tray. He'll have her prescriptions filled and wash the sheets and the quilts and stand on the back porch to pin them to the line. He'll keep the Ford gassed up in case she has a bad spell in the middle of the night and he has to get her into the city fast.

Soon after she dies he will search around through her things for the list of his sins, but he won't ever find it. He'll give her Bible and her other books back to the church she got them from. In a couple of years, he'll move in with a woman of limited means who was left alone about the same time he was. Her grown children will try hard to get used to him. Surprisingly, a few of the town people will bring modest wedding gifts to the door, a hand mixer, a cut-glass vase, a small framed *Blue Boy* done in petit point. Grady and the widow will pool their resources and live for a long time, quite happily and privately, in sin. Once or twice before he's too old to move Grady will pull her from her brocade chair and waltz her round the room, humming a sad old love tune he remembers from the lake to lend some rhythm to their steps.

NORM is married and his wife loves to dance. They've only missed one Casino dance in six years, and that was because of a wedding in Windsor they had to go to. He's heavyset and dark, he always looks like he could use a shave, although he shaves all the time. He wears whatever his wife puts out for him to wear; he figures she's the one who has to keep everything clean and ironed, she might as well tell him what to wear. He works for a small trucking company, he was never any scholar, and he makes big bucks; he likes to drive and he likes to drive long and hard. They already have a house half paid for, it's in her name in case anything should happen to him, and that's more than most guys his age have got. When he's gone on a three or four day haul, his wife sews things, curtains and clothes for the kids. Sometimes she sews for other people, she's that good, and she takes the money and banks it in her own account. He figures that's fair enough. Sometimes she uses some of her money to buy him expensive things he'd never ask for, a wool sweater, a soft leather wallet, an oak liquor cabinet for the living room. She likes quality.

Usually they go to the dances with another couple, people their age, people like them. They start out at home with maybe a barbecue supper and a few rye and Cokes and then, about nine o'clock, he picks up the sitter and they head out to the lake. There's some flirting around sometimes, high school stuff, but he doesn't get any ideas about any other women and nobody gets any ideas about his. That stuff's bullshit. Jaws get broken over that kind of stuff. What he's seen of it makes him sick. He likes his wife and he likes his kids and he likes his job. He figures that's more than enough.

At the Casino, he dances the first few with his wife and then he lets her go. Give her a summer night at the lake and she's sixteen all over again. She's happy, and later, she's still happy, laughing and brave on top of him in bed. He just hopes she can always dance. She often starts out with Jack, the skinny McLean kid, and Norm likes to watch him swing her around the floor, he likes to watch her make the kid feel good. When they're finished, Jack delivers her right back to Norm's side, although Norm always asks, Why bring her back, she won't stay. She carries on, dances with most of the other men from town. They consider her part of their evening, and when she takes them back to their wives she usually stays to talk for a bit. She remembers things. She can name everybody's kids, right down to the babies.

Norm tries to make a point of dancing with Donna and her friends. They used to do the babysitting and he knows most of their parents, one way or another. He always asks them, How's your lovelife, and often they try to confide in him, hinting at broken hearts and bullheaded boyfriends and dreams too complicated to come true. He tells them all, even the ones who aren't so pretty, that they're young and beautiful and that they shouldn't take any crap. He tells them if he were still a young stud on the prowl, he wouldn't have to look far. They laugh at the thought of him being a young stud and tell him he's just saying that and he says, No I'm not. Sometimes when he's holding one of the plainer girls, he can see a pretty rough time ahead for her and a low-grade sadness settles into his shoulders. When that happens, he'll hold on to her a little tighter than necessary, finger her back without letting on, pat her bum when the dance is finished and she's leaving him.

Once, when he was busy talking, one of the young Americans, a cocky type with a deep tan from waterskiing all the damn day long, asked his wife to dance. It was a slow dance and she kept backing away from him and looking at his face, talking to him. Then he said something she didn't like and she walked out of his arms and left him standing dumb in the middle of the floor. When Norm asked did she want to tell him exactly what had been said to her, she said not really. There was a brief grouping of men around Norm, which the kid picked right up on. He left with a couple of his buddies and didn't show his face again until the end of the summer.

NORM will grow older watching his wife dance and enjoying the benefits of her happiness a little later. Both of his kids will stay around home. They'll marry and bring their own kids over often, which will please Norm more than he can say, although he'll wish there was a little more discipline used. He'll tell his wife as long as he lives he'll never get used to backtalk from a kid. He'll have enough money to help set the grandkids up and he'll do it, although they won't show any recognizable signs of gratitude. I can wait, he'll say.

When he is fifty-eight, his wife will make a quick trip into the city for dress material one rainy summer afternoon and on the way home she'll be run off the road by a camper trying to pass a semi on a slippery curve.

Norm will bluff through another nineteen years, grieving every minute of every day of every year, pretending to be okay, putting people off. The most he'll say is, You have to keep going, don't you? At his granddaughter's wedding dance, the grateful bride will come to him after she's danced with her new husband and her father and coax him onto the floor, pulling on his arm, wrapping it around her waist. He'll tell her that she is young and beautiful and that she shouldn't take any crap.

THE CASINO will burn one Saturday night, right to the ground. The fire will start downstairs in some old, nearly bare wires and will be helped along by a nice breeze off the lake. A cottager will go to the mini-golf to call in the fire. No one will die, although the whole thing will go up like a cardboard box. None of the cops will be around when it starts, although one of them will be cruising the beach in his car and he'll get there soon, lights flashing, siren blaring.

Duncan, Jack, Grady and Norm will come together in a group at the top of the oak staircase and stand there herding people, holding back each wave of dancers until they think the stairs can take them. Everyone will go along with this. The fire won't be right under the stairs, but close enough. Grady will belt a couple of jerks who are horsing around, who think this is exciting. They'll sober right up. Norm's wife will want to stay with him, but he'll get her started on the stairs and she'll move down and out with the others. Duncan and Jack will help the band carry their instruments over to the top of the stairs and then Norm will lose it. Jesus, he'll yell, I think those can stay behind.

When everyone but the four of them and the band is down the stairs, Norm will feel the floor with his hands and shout to the others that he's taking one quick run around the balcony. They all know that a kid who's had too much will sometimes go out there to sleep it off for a while. Duncan and Jack will point to the balcony on the lakeside and tell him they'll check there. Grady will wait on the top step. They'll all come back coughing pretty bad, shaking their heads. Nobody, they'll say. Smoke will rise in soft thin streams through the dance floor and it will be hot, even through their shoes they'll feel it. Norm will say, All right, one at a time on these stairs, and they'll start down. Duncan will grab the fiddle, Jack will take the two guitars, and the men from the band will pick up the drums. You're last then, Norm will say. You're bringing those drums, you're behind me.

They'll make it, all of them, although when they get halfway down the stairs there will be nothing to see but black smoke and no way to hear anything but the fire. They'll turn in the direction they've turned a hundred times before and they'll find the open doors. They'll run through the parking lot and down the dune toward the crowd which has gathered on the beach: dancers and cottagers, children in their pyjamas, older people who were asleep. Lights will be on in all the cottages. Duncan will give the fiddle back to the fiddler. Jack will drop both guitars in the sand and sit down beside the drums. They'll all cough hard and hawk to clear their lungs.

The parking lot will be empty of all cars but Norm's Pontiac and Duncan's Dad's Buick. Five guys will get the Pontiac in neutral and push it back as far as they can, trying to stay off the road because they can hear the fire truck coming, maybe a mile away, but coming. A few others will run over to the Buick, but it's been sitting pretty close to the heat and the paint is already starting to shine funny, starting to darken and blister.

Just before the fire truck pulls up, the piano will go through, hitting the cement floor like nothing else could. Down near the water, the piano player will quietly say, That was an F chord if I'm not mistaken, and there will be small chuckles all around him, although he won't laugh.

When the firemen jump down from the truck, Norm and Grady will be there to tell them that there's nobody inside, everybody's out. Several of the firemen will haul a thick hose down to the lake and set up a portable pump. When they get the water coming they'll quickly put the hose to the Buick and then turn their attention to the Casino. They'll lay on lots of water and nobody will know why.

The Casino owners will arrive, two guys from the city who stay with their families in rented cottages all summer, and they'll be happy as hell to hear that no one was hurt in any way. Grady will ask them if she was insured, and one of them will say yeah. When Grady asks how much, they'll just ignore him, but he knows he'll find out eventually. People tend to tell him things.

Parents will start to arrive, the word having got to town. They'll park way back on the Casino road, and it will take them a while to make their way through the firemen and down to the beach to find whoever belongs to them. Two carloads will arrive from the reserve which borders the cottages a couple of miles down the lake to the south, and a few army people will come from the camp on the north end, but there won't be anything for them to do.

Some people will leave, the very young, the very old, but most will stay. Although the air directly above the Casino will hold the yellow-red glow of the fire, the moon and the stars and the silvery sheen on the surface of the water will be eclipsed by smoke. Men will get flashlights from their glove boxes. They'll aim them like searchlights up to the fire and over the surrounding dunes, out across the dark water, down to their feet if they're walking from one cluster of people to another, the light cutting a safe path through the darkness, through the unexpected driftwood. Lake Huron will move generously through the thick fire hose all night long. The wind will change, pushing the heat down to the beach. Large cinders will drift through the air, coming to rest on the sand and on the water, on heads and shoulders and arms and on the cars which were moved from the lot and parked haphazardly on the shore. The roof will fall in around two-thirty and the last wall will go just as the sun's coming up.

Jack and Duncan will send their parents, who have driven out to find them, home. They will wander around the dark beach all night, talking to their friends and to older people they've never talked to before, easing themselves into the circle of girls who have built a small fire on the beach with the driest of the driftwood and kindling borrowed from a nearby cottage.

In the morning they'll catch a ride back to town with Grady in his truck. The Buick will have to be towed in. While he's got them, Grady will decide to tell them a few war stories; this isn't the first fire he's seen and not the biggest, not by a country mile. They'll sit quiet. They won't hear half of what he's saying to them.

Norm will stand down on the beach with his wife most of the night, watching. He'll wander off occasionally to talk to someone and then he'll come back and stand behind her, wrap his arms around her, hold as much of her as he can to try to stop the shivering. Eventually, she'll remember home. She'll tell Norm the sitter's probably good and scared, likely wondering what happened to them. Then she'll tell herself that the kid is more than smart enough to have called her mother, she'll know by now. Norm will smooth her hair with his hand and tell her that they'll find some place else to dance.

At dawn, they'll drive home tired. In the car, she will tell him that she saw a few fair-sized rats in the dunes when she was running down to the beach, and Norm will say that makes sense if you think about it. When they're almost home he'll tell her he's pretty sure it was the balcony that made it go up so fast, all that air getting sucked in, feeding the fire. He won't tell her that his feet are burning, that they still feel hot inside his shoes. He won't even know if it's heat he feels or just the memory of heat.

FIGURINES

The figurines, a prepubescent boy and girl, are a foot high and hollow. The boy wears a creamy white sailor top, blue britches and a dusty, wide-brimmed country hat. His strawberry blond hair is very long and thick. He stands holding an upright oar, hugging it close to his body, his eyes fixed on some puzzling middle distance. The girl, plump by today's standards and fairly self-assured by the set of her jaw, is dressed in a summer frock with a dropped waist. A voluptuous satin sash encircles her hips. In the crook of her elbow she holds, too tightly, a half-crushed nosegay. Her hair, the colour of pale beach sand, is longer still and thicker, falling heavily on her shoulders.

Joan imagines these children to be cousins, on an outing near a sun-dappled lake.

The clay, painted by a steady hand in summer white and soft pastels, blue and pink and apple green, and a fleshy peach, could be from anywhere. The figurines are not attributable to anyone or to any time. There are no markings on the bases and this disappoints Joan, more than seems reasonable.

She's stood the cousins on a high glass shelf in her curio, just under the lights. There is a good chance her dinner guests see them as coy artifacts from some impossible past and, of course, they are.

The figurines had been a gift to Joan's great-aunt Lottie when she was a young, unmarried nurse. This would have been in the early twenties, the reputedly Roaring Twenties when there were women in the world who eagerly grabbed the opportunity after a God-awful war to be frivolous, who drank bathtub gin and danced unrestrained in dresses layered with fringes that snapped out from their bodies in waves. The aunt lived in with a family while the aged father died, tending to him. She told Joan this. He must have needed what only a nurse could administer to ease him through it, something from a pharmacist, something potent but dangerous in the wrong hands. Whatever his need, Joan imagines her aunt fulfilling it with the same detached care she displayed in very late middle age, when she knew her. When the work was completed, the figurines were given to her, either in payment or above payment, in gratitude.

The figurines do not convey any particular sense of the aunt's character. You would not imagine any connection between her and these elegant clay children unless you saw them, as Joan did, sitting on a gate-legged oak table in her aunt's living room, just behind a cut-glass humbug dish. They had been a gift and she'd taken them and incorporated them into her life. That's what people like her did with gifts. She would not have thought to ask if she could perhaps exchange them for something a little more to her liking. It's possible that they had not been purchased for her at all but were esteemed family possessions. It's possible that they had been a gift another time, valued and held in good keeping, and then given again.

Joan has no idea what her aunt recalled when she looked at the figurines. Perhaps her patient had died independently, taking care to keep the biggest part of the task for himself, resisting the need to make demands when no one with a good heart could refuse him. Perhaps there were children who brought her tea after her nap and asked if they could touch her hair. It's equally possible that she disliked the family. The room they'd assigned to her might have been cold, the blankets rough, the children precociously rude. Although Joan could be angry if she believed her aunt was badly treated, there was no hint one way or the other.

When Joan was young, she saw her Aunt Lottie once a week, every week of every year, when her family picked her up for church on Sunday and delivered her gratefully home again. And she was there with them for Christmas, just off to the side, out of the way in her chair by the buffet, smiling quickly at passing children, running her fingers whenever she could through a thick head of hair, and largely ignoring the kitchen work. She behaved like a guest, a skill Joan has always admired.

Often on Sunday mornings Joan was sent from the back seat of the car to her aunt's front door to tell her they'd arrived, and sometimes she would be told to sit in the living room for a minute while her aunt searched for mislaid summer gloves or a book she'd promised one of her friends at church, history usually. Joan was always invited to help herself to a humbug and she always did, pulling one sticky piece from the others, replacing the cut-glass lid gingerly, aware of noise and the possibility of shattered glass. Above the figurines, hung high on the wall, high enough to prompt Joan to lift her head to read it, the Serenity Prayer was offered in a framed petit point sampler. The sampler had been a going-away gift from a woman friend on the occasion of the aunt's leaving Ontario to move out West with her husband and son, when she was young. Perhaps hoping to ensure an easy understanding of the prayer's power, the friend who had worked the needle had purposefully enlarged each letter of the five main words: GOD, GRACE, SERENITY, COURAGE, WISDOM. Sitting beside the figurines, sucking on a humbug, Joan generously granted an appropriateness to the prayer, because her aunt was old, because she had been weakened.

Her aunt had been widowed early, and Joan doesn't know how she lived or who took care of her financially, although someone must have. There were no pension plans available then, no big insurance policies on the lives of men who might die young. The husband, John, had had a farm in Ontario, which he'd sold off when they made their move to the West, some time in the late twenties. There was a son, Billy, and Joan thinks she remembers pictures of him, at five or six, wearing short wool pants and good dark shoes, bright looking, with the prairie behind him as a backdrop. But maybe she's never seen his picture. Perhaps she's confused him with other boys in short wool pants and good shoes who were placed against a backdrop of crops for their pictures. Billy drowned in the West, in a slough, although Joan knows nothing about the circumstances. She doesn't know if he was wild and headstrong, forever beyond the reach of his mother's protective hands, or dreamy and clumsy, given to wandering off and forgetting to come back for his midday meal. She does know they returned to Ontario almost immediately after his drowning. Joan's father once told her, riding in a car somewhere with his felt hat between them on the seat, that he'd always had a good deal of respect for John, for his determination to go out West and break new ground. He said there wasn't land enough for third sons at home, that what looked like choice wasn't always choice. He said when they came back to Ontario, they came pretty much empty-handed and that arrangements had to be made to get them resettled. Joan's father often conjured up these scattered segments of history, composing as much for himself as for anyone else his own inter-pretation of distant events, pulling details forward to give the past a present shape. It was like a hobby.

So John did farm again, on somebody's land. He lived for a while after they went back to Ontario, before Lottie became middle-aged and then old, searching for mislaid summer gloves while the church bells rang all over town and Joan sat in a straight-backed chair eating her humbugs, glancing up occasionally at the Serenity Prayer, touching, more than once, her figurines.

Lottie brought the figurines West, she packed them and brought them with her on the train. The idea was to leave for good, to make a new home. And she took them back to Ontario with her when it was over, although there is not much evidence of movement, Joan can find only two insignificant chips.

Joan was out West herself by the time her aunt was elderly. She went home to Ontario only occasionally, and during one of these visits her father obliquely insisted that she accompany him to the seniors' home where the aunt lived. Joan didn't know who had moved her, or how it played out, although her sister-in-law was a volunteer there. Her father, a man of convention and regularity, continued to make it a habit to see Aunt Lottie every Sunday, as he had through all the other years. She was well into her seventies and her mind was wild with Alzheimer's, but her body had stayed fairly sound. Joan was twenty-two, full of herself and stupid enough to think her aunt might be interested in her travels. As she walked with her father up the sidewalk toward the wide double doors, he counselled her just to smile and not to take her aunt up on anything she might say.

It's unlikely that Joan could have found her on her own, although they had her properly dressed, her two rings still on her fingers, her lips a pale, respectable pink. They had placed her in a wheelchair, tied her upright with soft thick bands of bleached white cloth, although that's the visitor talking, they would not have been soft from her perspective. She didn't know them, they did not live in the world her mind recognized. Only once or twice did she call Joan's father by his own name.

She was beyond self-discipline and rude, to Joan's father, to the other patients, to the nurses and doctors who stopped to touch her shoulder and speak to them. She used language that Joan imagined to be new to her, mumbling saucy remarks in response to any attention she received. She was boastful. She talked of running a hospital single-handedly, surrounded by lazy idiots who would not take their responsibilities seriously. Joan's father forged on, spoke to her courteously, steered her when he could. He addressed her as he would have had her mind been sound, nodding during the brief moments when she seemed to be in control, ignoring the bitter tangents as he might have ignored harmless forks of lightning. When he told her that Joan lived in the West now, she strained forward in her chair and responded with a sharp hatred for the prairie, said it was so blessed big you couldn't find anything, couldn't be heard above the filthy wind. "Damn the godforsaken prairie," she said, squinting, looking to Joan for complicity.

Joan's father had said they would stay an hour and they did. They drank the coffee offered by a volunteer and they each took a generous piece of fruit bread from a silver tray. Joan's sister-in-law was busy elsewhere, but she came over once and stood behind the wheelchair, wrapped her arms around Lottie's shoulders and kissed her hair. This gesture prompted a shy grin to break across the closed, puzzled face.

When the hour was over and they were in the car, Joan asked her father had she really run a hospital somewhere and he said yes she had, a small one, they were all small then, and many of them were run by women not unlike her. He said she'd been a strong and capable and responsible young woman, words which Joan took as comment on her own activities, as well as context for the dated obscenities they'd heard. She laughed and said good for her. She repeated one of the milder phrases her aunt had used with such panache. She said, "Maybe she's been a lady too long." She said, "Good for you, Aunt Lottie." Her father tried to laugh, reluctant to push Joan farther away than she'd already gone, but then he turned his face from her, as he had not once turned from his aunt. "No," he said. "It has not been good for her. It has rarely been good for her."

Joan did not go back to Ontario for her aunt's funeral; it's not possible to make the trip for every death. Lottie was rarely in her thoughts. She had her own small children. Their needs and the necessities which bounced off the walls of the house kept her, as they say, busy.

And then Joan's mother died. She went East and stayed for a while, claiming her share of the grief, taking her part of the work made necessary by death. As is the custom, people congregated at her parents' house, coming in without knocking, carrying practical casseroles wrapped in newspaper and still-warm baking, leaving sometimes in the middle of a sentence if a chair was needed. Someone, a young neighbour Joan didn't know, raked the lawn. There was talk, in contrived, ordinary language, of the distribution of her mother's belongings, which her father allowed and encouraged; nearly everyone connected to her mother, and she had many friends, valued something. Joan refused to take part in these discussions. She sat in all the rooms, she walked from room to room, she picked up the things her mother had accumulated and put them down again where she had placed them. When she saw the figurines in her mother's living room, she saw nothing.

Not very long after her mother's death, Joan's father shipped a sturdy cardboard box West to her. The box was full of the things her mother had named hers, the naming done on a small piece of masking tape stuck to the bottom of each item, the name Joan clear in her mother's weakened script. The first thing out was a feathery crystal dinner bell which, as her father indicated in an enclosed note, had been a wedding gift from good friends who used to travel with them to Florida, friends long since gone. There was a Royal Doulton grandmother and a few pieces of silver, a pickle cruet, and a magnificent lace tablecloth which Joan remembered fingering nervously as a child sitting at the dinner table. At the bottom of the box, because of their weight, and enclosed separately in their own bubble wrap, were the figurines. They'd come West a second time. As the executor of a woman whose mind no longer gave witness to her history or her character or her accomplishments, Joan's father had apparently arranged that these clay children come like a gift from his aunt to them, first to Joan's mother, and now to her.

His note listing the contents of the box told Joan that she had asked for the figurines the last time she saw her aunt. Did she remember?

Joan did not remember asking and she thought it was pretty nervy if she had. She wondered if her father might have imagined this request, or if he had simply decided that something which should have been true, was true. Not content with wanting her to have the figurines, he wanted her to want them.

She repacked the box from Ontario, carried it upstairs and pushed it to the back of the spare room closet. She has accumulated more than enough on her own over the years, selecting things carefully, placing them deliberately, her taste becoming more and more selective, more and more trustworthy. Uncomfortable with disarray and pleased with her pragmatism, she'd long ago sold the wedding gifts that no longer suited her at a neighbourhood garage sale, remembering the giver briefly as she washed and priced each item.

But her father, who with his habits and regularity and his packing of boxes has become death's familiar, has been joined in his small campaign by Joan's son, who is oblivious but no less insistent. These two men, very young and very old, have conspired against her, closed in around her middle age, their lives brushing hers if she moves.

Her son took *his* place this past summer at Waskesiu, when Joan was sitting halfway up the hill searching through the binoculars for her husband and their daughters, who were out on the lake in a rented boat fishing. With an unintended and only slight shift of her hands she found not them but him. He stood on the shore absolutely still, as if posed, hugging one of the paddles from his inflatable raft, his eyes fixed on some puzzling middle distance. He stood long-haired and lanky and sunburned, his arms and legs caked with sand, his face dazed with exhaustion and accomplishment. Perhaps it was only the evening air between them, between his position down on the sand at the edge of the water and hers on the hill under the poplars. Perhaps it was only a quirk in her brain, one image among the millions stored and ready taking a deep breath and jumping the empty space between one brain cell and another.

Joan is not exactly unhappy about the conspiracy. She has adjusted. In the fall, on a quick trip downtown for towels, she found and bought a honey-coloured oak curio, irresponsibly using the money that should have gone to overdue income tax or a paint job for the roof. Her curio has leaded panes, and, inside, two recessed lights. It's quite big, it crowds everything else in the dining room, but it holds a lot. The feathery crystal bell is on display, and the Royal Doulton grandmother, and the pickle cruet and the slightly tarnished silver. The figurines sit on their own glass shelf just under the lights, turned one toward the other; pale children stranded in innocence.

And, worse, she has begun to ask certain people if they will leave her things, specific things, named and identified as gifts to her in their wills. She is not nearly brave enough to depend on chance. Just before her brother died of a hard, hard cancer, when they both knew it would be the last time she would be able to ask him anything at all, she asked if she could please have something. And, "Yes," he'd said, "I want you to have something, just tell me what you'd like." She picked a small, surprisingly heavy glass box which he'd had for years. She keeps it on a butternut chest in her bedroom. It holds the stones she's stolen from other continents.

And she's willing to let her aged father's lawyer worry about his Bell Canada shares and whatever else there is; she has no doubt it will be fairly distributed according to her father's directions, which are none of her business. What she wants is his battered Testament. He has used his Testament, for a long time and unapologetically, as a place for private dialogue; the margins are full of thoughts and doubts and possibilities, question marks. Joan expects to find evolution in these thoughts and doubts and possibilities, which she thinks she could track by the diminishing strength of his hand. She expects to find hope and disillusionment and stamina and heartache. She expects to find clues. When she asked for the Testament during a Sunday phone call, he made her listen for a minute to dead air. He said he'd see; he said she wasn't the only one interested.

And she's looked around. Late in the night when the house is quiet, she has allowed herself to wonder what she will leave, and who might want to lay a claim. Who, for instance, might want those stones she's stolen from other continents? Who might want the glass box that holds them? Her books? The jade ring she bought with her first kids-all-in-school paycheque in a narrow hole-in-the-wall estate jewellery store in

Vancouver? Her mother's feathery crystal dinner bell? The coy figurines, which are still, given the distances travelled, almost pristine? The battered, annotated Testament, if it does one day come into her waiting hands?

PATSY FLATER'S BRIEF SEARCH FOR GOD

1: ETERNAL LIFE

Sometimes after the Monday night children's meeting at the Gospel Hall Patsy walked down to the creek behind the canning factory to check on the pickles. There were three barrels of them huddled on the surface of the frozen creek, they'd been there since the ice got hard enough to hold them. It was some experiment, an idea that two acquaintances of her father's had come up with. He called them entrepreneurs, although not to their faces. Patsy didn't know what the pickles were supposed to do over the winter, maybe just make it through until spring, emerging from the barrels hard and crisp and sweet like her mother's gherkins, which had been done up properly in sealers and stored in the cold cellar in the basement at home.

On clear nights, if she felt warm, she would sit on the slope of the bank, lean back and stare up through the bare branches of the scrub maples at the dark sky and the stars and the cold winter moon. Sometimes she would lie right down and fan her arms and legs through the crusty snow to make an angel's imprint.

Other times she walked the dark streets from the Gospel Hall to her house slowly, taking different routes, stopping in her tracks to stare in a window if she saw something rare or unique: a bird loose from a cage, a fight, people embracing. Occasionally she walked with Eleanor. Eleanor was made to go to the children's meetings by her bootlegger dad, who was able to earn, given the town fathers' commitment to keeping the town dry, a dependable living off the town sons. Eleanor was bravely blasphemous all the way home, making up absurd Bible verses, getting off lines of derision, giggling, snorting. She said the kids at the meetings were easy pickings, and so were the men up front.

Patsy's sisters, who were quite a bit older, hadn't gone to the children's meetings. It wasn't compulsory. Her parents neither discouraged nor urged Patsy to go. She just went. She was collecting Testaments.

The Gospel Hall was light red brick with white double doors and plain in comparison to the United Church or the Presbyterian or the Baptist, which was Patsy's church. The pews were pale golden oak and sturdy, they had been built square cornered, without decorative curves. The pulpit was just a very high table with a chair behind it and the glass in the narrow windows along each side of the hall had been frosted but not stained, there were no biblical figures pieced together with small bits of glass. The walls were cream coloured and on every wall there were framed pictures of Jesus, either head and shoulders or full body in a white robe, with his face glowing, with women or children at his feet.

Patsy knew some of the children who attended the meetings from school, a few went to her church, some were farm kids who were brought in especially on Monday nights. They were all very young. The man who spoke to the children was Patsy's mother's second cousin, he had the same last name as her grandmother, Watson, although his branch had got separated, she'd never seen him at any family gatherings. She saw him only on Monday nights from the November she was ten until the following February, never before, and never after.

The meetings always started with attendance and then singing. There was a piano at the front, played by a thin and energetic woman Patsy didn't know, whose voice was not as strong as she assumed it was. Mr. Watson was helped by an assistant who had a clear tenor voice and led them with hearty enthusiasm through the children's hymns: "Jesus Loves the Little Children," and "Jesus Loves Me," and "He's the Lily of the Valley" and, near Christmas, some of the carols Patsy liked to sing. After the singing, there were games, contests.

If you were chosen to stand up and recite the names of the books of the Old or the New Testaments, you could win a pastel bookmark, blue or green or mauve or yellow or pink. At the top of each bookmark there was a gentle scene featuring lambs or flowers or children and below this a Bible verse written out in small script. If you could recite the books of either of the Testaments backwards, you got two bookmarks. If you had memorized correctly the verses assigned by Mr. Watson the previous week, you got still more, and when you'd earned enough, and if you had perfect attendance, you were presented with a child's Testament. These were white leather, soft and small, very easy for a child to hold. If you held your Testament tightly closed, the edging on the pages could lead you to believe that inside each thin page was dark red.

Patsy quickly established herself as a dependable voice for a fast and precise naming of the books of the Bible, forwards or backwards. She took pride in a perfect recitation, or an exact rendering of a verse; she liked leaving her pew and going to the front to retrieve her winnings. By the end of it all she had five Testaments. The other children made no secret of the fact that they thought this was unfair, but she didn't care. She thought if they'd wanted to make it fair, they would have just handed everything out. She kept her Testaments with other treasures in a skate box under her bed, a place she assumed her mother didn't check.

After the contests Mr. Watson gave his talk, which was never very pleasant. He started out standing at the pulpit and then paced back and forth from one side of the room to the other, pausing to make eye contact with some of the children, sometimes stopping to touch one of them on the shoulder. He held his zippered black Bible tight in his hand, raising it high in the air and shaking it when he wanted to make a point. His voice had a granular edge to it, and he knew how to make the children listen. He held them by pushing the pitch of his words high and suddenly dropping it low again, and by alternately whispering and shouting. As he talked the children settled, their ordinary fidgeting ceased.

He said his only concern was their eternal lives. He had long studied the Bible and he knew, oh, he knew what lay ahead for the children if they did not take Jesus Christ as their own personal saviour. He painted cruel pictures with his voice so they'd know. There would be darkness blacker than night, and foul, monstrous creatures and a wide rushing river of fire. Sinners would crowd together in search of comfort. Flames would lick at their flesh forever and there would be no death to release them. "There is no mystery," he would shout. "It's all here for us in Revelation, if only we'd listen."

It didn't take long for the church to become crowded

with his exotic images, and Patsy often had to resist the urge to run to the back of the room and turn off all the lights. He created a Hell so exact and vibrant that she would easily be able to picture it for the rest of her life. He had information about Heaven as well, which he always held back until the end, soothing them with promises.

In February, Mr. Watson got sick for a while and two of the people who helped him, tall, lank men with long necks and prominent Adam's apples, gave the talks. They worked as a team and they weren't nearly as good as Mr. Watson, although they used more or less the same words. Partly to fill the time, they introduced an opportunity for questions at the end of their talks, something Mr. Watson would not have done, and Patsy took the chance to ask the question she'd been sitting with for quite some time. Was everybody who didn't attend the Gospel Hall doomed? She was confident the answer would be no, she expected a short, complicated discussion about exceptions and second chances, the proof found somewhere in all those pages, all those verses, but she got a surprise. Unfortunately, she was told, and wasn't it sad, wasn't it truly sad, everyone else was going to go to Hell, it was clear in the Word of God. She put up her hand again, holding it firmly up as she waited through several questions about Lazarus and the woman at the well, and when one of the men finally nodded at her, Patsy asked him would her friend from school who went to the Roman Catholic church spend eternity in Hell? There was sincere regret in the man's voice when he answered her and then he brightened. "You can witness," he said. "You could save her." After the meeting Patsy walked straight home, with Eleanor, who told her she was pretty stupid if she didn't see that coming.

For a while she would leave the house on Monday nights and only pretend to go to the meetings. She stopped instead at the creek to sit near the barrels of pickles or wandered the cold streets on the lookout for rare or unique human activity. Finally, she just stayed home. When her mother asked why she wasn't going any more, Patsy said, "Because they're all crazy." Her mother said she was afraid that was a distinct possibility, although normally she would have outlawed any such talk. Family, even the most distant of cousins, was always to be given the benefit of the doubt, the worst that could be said being nothing at all, a silence when a name was mentioned, to allow each listener a private bit of time to remember the reason for the absence of words.

The five white Testaments stayed in the skate box under Patsy's bed through years of dustings until she packed up for university, when her mother turned her room into a sometime guest room, emptying a few drawers, moving the furniture round. Patsy never asked what she did with them.

2: GRACE

Patsy's friend Carol, who was Roman Catholic, had an uncle who was in an iron lung. Sunday afternoons were often used by families for short car trips to visit people and on one of these afternoons Patsy accepted an invitation from Carol's mother to visit the uncle. She said his town was only forty minutes away and they would easily be back by supper time. One of the things Patsy valued about having friends was getting to know the people who surrounded them: rude older brothers, grandfathers who would sometimes talk another language, crazy aunts who visited from Sudbury. She accepted the invitation without calling her parents, there was nothing unusual about a trip to see somebody, and they got into the car and started down the highway. Patsy sat in the front beside Carol, at the window. The snow was almost gone from the fields and the highway was dark and dry. Carol's mother said she liked a dry highway.

They hadn't got very far when Carol's mother asked if Patsy knew what an iron lung was. Patsy answered no, she didn't, trying to make her voice sound ready for an explanation. She wasn't told much about iron lungs but she did hear about the uncle. Carol's mother said that he had been a normal, active boy like other boys and then when he was twelve he got very sick. He had to spend a long time in the hospital in the city and then he came home with his iron lung, which was smaller than the big hospital lungs, designed for home use. She said children were safer now, with all the vaccines. She said he had always been smart, and interested in what went on. She said he liked visitors.

The house where the uncle lived was really the grand-mother's house, one of those narrow yellow-brick houses with a side porch, just like a farmhouse, but built in town. When they pulled into the driveway, the grandmother was already on the porch ready to greet them, drying her hands on the tea towel she had tucked into the belt of her navy blue wool dress. She had hugs for everyone except Patsy, but she smiled a generous smile and put her hand firmly on Patsy's shoul-der, guiding her in and through the front room straight to the kitchen, where the table was set with tea and bread and butter plates and a tin of fresh cookies, oatmeal and maca-roons and hermits. There was a door off the kitchen to a bed-room, and hanging beside the door against green wallpaper, a repeated diagonal pattern of small faded tea kettles, there was a crucifix, similar to the one above the sofa in Carol's living room. Patsy didn't much like the Catholic cross, she preferred the empty Protestant cross because it was evidence that Jesus was gone, risen, but she was getting used to the twisted figure, she could see that it worked as a reminder.

Standing in the kitchen with her hands on the back of a chair, Patsy could hear the uncle quietly calling "Hello, Hello," and "Get in here." They walked in and gathered around his bed, which was a high hospital bed. He looked middle-aged to Patsy, like a parent. He reached to take his sister's hands in his own and she leaned down to kiss him. Carol approached and stretched to put her cheek on his and then she stood back and said, "This is my friend Patsy."

He made a great fuss with his arms and with the muscles in his face. His voice was raspy, but strong enough. He said, "You, I've heard about," and he laughed and then they all laughed together. Patsy could smell shaving cream in the air, and she saw that his pyjama bottoms were fresh and had been ironed.

The lung enclosed him from his armpits to just below his waist. It looked like a magician's box, except that it was round and made of iron, and there were windows and dials and controls and hoses and a steady, mechanical noise and a sturdy cord which was plugged into the wall at the foot of the bed. There was a chair beside the bed piled high with thick newspapers from the city, and a dictionary. On the other side of the bed there was a shelf nailed into the wall, which held a radio and some paper and pens and a pair of scissors. On the wall above his head there was another crucifix, the same twisted figure, the same matted hair under the crown of thorns, the same face turned down and away.

Carol's mother indicated that the girls should go back to the kitchen, so they went out to the table and sat down with

Carol's grandmother. She poured them tea and gave them each a bread and butter plate for their cookies and a small embroidered napkin. She asked them about school, she wanted to know exactly where they were in each of their subjects, geography especially, and was that odd man with the sports car still principal? She wanted to know all about their teachers, she hoped they were good and strict. "Listen to me now," she said. "You'll thank them." Patsy could hear quiet talk from the bedroom, not many separate words but talk, most of it from Carol's uncle. After a while Carol's mother came out for a cup of tea and nodded to the girls that they should go in again. Carol took Patsy's hand and she got up and followed her into the room, walking to the foot of the bed where there was a space to sit but Carol caught her eye just in time and gave her head a quick, almost imperceptible shake, so Patsy stood where she was. Carol pushed the newspapers and the dictionary from the chair to the floor so she could sit down, and then her uncle told her to get last Saturday's *Star* from the mess she'd just made and find the crossword puzzle. He said they'd had a dickens of a time with it and he had been waiting for someone younger and smarter to come along. Although his hands were strong and he used them freely, Patsy noticed that the tips of some of his fingers were gone, and that his legs were very thin, and that his feet didn't fill his socks. Carol found the newspaper and opened it to the puzzle. There were only two words not solved. One of the clues was "Soldier for hire (9)," and as soon as Carol read it out, Patsy knew the answer.

"Mercenary," she said, pleased.

Carol's uncle said, "Yes, indeed," and he reached to his shelf and handed Carol a pen. "Fill that in," he said.

The second clue was "Pungent (5)." Carol shrugged her shoulders, she'd played this game before, but Patsy closed her eyes hard to think. She couldn't get it. "What letters have you got?" she asked.

Carol read out, "*A*, blank, *R*, blank, *D*."

"Damn," Patsy said. "I don't know it."

"Watch your mouth there," the uncle said. "Just keep thinking. Give it a day or two."

Carol's mother stood leaning against the door-frame drinking tea, and before she could stop herself she said, "Acrid. It's acrid, isn't it?"

When it was time to go Patsy stood back while the others kissed him goodbye, wondering if she would be expected to take a turn. And then she just got ready and did it. He laughed when she approached him and she could feel his hand briefly on her neck, grateful and cold.

They backed out the driveway and when they got onto the highway Carol and her mother began to talk about other things, an upcoming shopping trip to the city, a winter coat that could not be let down and might as well be given to a cousin. Patsy stared at the mottled fields, at the fence posts and the fat black crows resting somehow on the barbed wire.

They dropped her off at home just before supper and it didn't come until she was sitting at the table listening to her father say grace, thanking God for their food. It came full force, it was so bad she had to leave the table. Her mother, who had already seen one girl through adolescence and its attendant, sudden heartaches, would normally have just let her go but she remembered that she had no knowledge at all about how Patsy had spent the afternoon and she followed her up the stairs, leaving the rest of the family puzzled but unwilling to let their suppers get cold. She sat sidesaddle on Patsy's bed and said, "You'd better tell me." She waited, mute, until she heard the uncle's name and then she put her hand on Patsy's forehead, pushing her bangs off her face back into her longer hair. It was a gesture she had been using with success most of her adult life. It had never before been refused.

3: CRUCIFIXION

Two years later, six weeks before Christmas, Patsy's mother and father decided to make their annual trip into the city for presents. Patsy was allowed to invite Carol and, as on other excursions, the two of them split off and shopped for a while on their own. They shared the cost of a *Seventeen* magazine and they searched out and found a special kind of ankle sock they couldn't get at home and they bought soft tartan head scarves, which were to be worn loose over their heads like shawls, the tasselled ends thrown back carelessly over their shoulders. They had lunch at a Chinese restaurant, where they shared an egg roll and an oval plate of sweet-and-sour pork, and when they had finished and got their fortune cookies, which were vague but quite satisfactory, they walked down the decorated street toward the theatres, stopping in every store alcove for a few minutes to stare through the glass and choose the best ring, the best sweater, the best pair of shoes. Then they lined up for the movie. They had picked *Spartacus*, with Kirk Douglas.

Throughout the movie, in which there was more flesh exposed than either of them had ever seen, not counting the pale familiar flesh they'd seen at home and at the beach, Carol behaved outrageously. "He's such a hunk," she said, lowering herself in the plush seat, and again and again, loudly, grabbing Patsy's arm, "Oh, he is such a hunk." During one of the love scenes, a woman behind them who wore a bright red coat with a big fox collar rapped her hard on the head and whispered, "Stop that."

"Battleaxe," Carol muttered, and carried right on.

It was dark when they emerged from the theatre. The city streets, wet and bright with Christmas lights strung up on store fronts, were full of tired women in heavy coats lugging home full shopping bags, their families' Christmas in the making, still boxed. As prearranged, the girls met Patsy's parents for a smorgasbord supper at the Iroquois Hotel. They each had the three-dollar special, all the jumbo shrimp they wanted and pink roast beef with corn fritters instead of Yorkshire pudding.

In the car on the way home the girls sat in the back seat with the *Seventeen* and Patsy's mother's new penlight, examining and making judgements on the sophisticated images, each confidently choosing outfits or hairstyles that would be perfect for the other. Patsy's father, quickly sick to death of all the talk about clothes and hair, caught Patsy's eyes in his rearview mirror and asked what the movie was about.

Carol pushed her elbow deep into Patsy's ribs and rolled her eyes, her face locked into her *oh, if he only knew* expression but Patsy quickly put on a fierce *not now* look.

"Gladiators," Patsy said. "And slaves. They had an uprising against the Romans. Kirk Douglas was the leader."

"Did the good guys win?" he asked.

Patsy gave a fair account. "At the end, Spartacus and his wife had a son," she said, "who would grow up free. But

Spartacus himself died on the cross. And there was a big battle, the Roman soldiers trapped the slaves down at the bottom of Italy. Afterwards the bodies were all piled up like coats on a bed."

"'Twas ever thus," her father said, giving his attention back to the road.

Carol stayed overnight. When they got up to Patsy's room, the first thing she did was close the door and dig her rosary out of her coat pocket. She knelt quietly against the high bed and eased the beads one at a time through her fingers, moving her lips quickly as she said her Hail Marys. To pass the time, Patsy unwrapped the tartan scarves and the ankle socks and placed them in separate piles on her dresser. When Carol was finished, they climbed into bed with the *Seventeen* but it wasn't long before Carol picked up where she'd left off with Kirk Douglas. She had no precise words to explain herself. She started sentences and left them unfinished. She said, "When she was swimming naked . . ." and "When they were lying on the grass talking about the wind . . ." and "When he put his hands on her stomach to feel the baby . . ." She sighed and tossed around in the bed to give some movement to her thoughts, moaning theatrically about the deep dimple in his chin, opening her arms to the room. She said it was easy to understand why someone would want to do it with a man like that.

She noticed eventually that Patsy wasn't giving her anything back, wasn't even listening. "What's with you?" she asked.

"Did you know they crucified everyone?" Patsy asked.

"What?" Carol said.

Patsy sat up in the bed. "I thought they only did that to Jesus."

"You thought they dreamt it up just for him?" Carol asked.

She picked up the *Seventeen* and began to leaf again through the glossy ads, lingering over a red angora sweater. "There are pictures of Christ with a thief on each side. One of the thieves even says something, doesn't he?" She shrugged her shoulders. "That's what they did then."

"I knew about the thieves," Patsy said. "I just didn't think there was anyone else. I thought the thieves were there so Jesus wouldn't be alone, or to make a better story. But they did it to everybody. All the time."

"Just to the men." Carol said. "I think women usually got stoned by their friends and neighbours."

"I thought that was the only time ever," Patsy said.

"What difference does it make?" Carol said. "The point is that he was the Son of God. He took all of our sins. That's the point."

Patsy had nothing to say. It wasn't the first time she had tripped on something everyone else had always seen. She fluffed her pillow and leaned back into it, pulled the quilts up to her chin. Carol threw the magazine off the bed and did the same. They both turned a few times and each finally slept her own sleep. Carol's dreams were enriched by the muscles in Kirk Douglas's arms and back and thighs, and by glances from his cool blue eyes. The afternoon movie had expelled her like a birth into young lusty womanhood and she was full term.

Patsy's dreams rolled through the night like hills. On every hill there were a hundred crosses and on every cross a man, his face turned down and away, his body twisted with its own weight. At the base of each cross friends and family sat quietly on the ground, mostly women sharing a bit of food, ready for the death, sticking it out. Soldiers in helmets and dark tunics who carried shotguns like her Uncle Peter's stood together in small groups talking and laughing. A few broke off and strolled alone through the rows of crosses. The hills rolled on forever and the colour of the sky was constant, a dull godless orange.

4: BAPTISM

When Patsy came to the age of decision, it was understood that she would be baptized. Baptism was compulsory. Unlike Carol, who had once unfolded from a cedar chest the lacy white infant's gown she'd worn the day the priest sprinkled her forehead with water and ensured her salvation, Patsy had lived the first part of her life at some risk. In her church infants were taken to the front and dedicated, not baptized. Parents and everyone else in the congregation were expected to stand up and promise to help the child live a good life; if the child died, there was the hope that God would understand. Baptism was for later, when you were old enough to think for yourself. It was supposed to be an act of the individual will. It wouldn't work otherwise. Six years earlier, when she was small, Patsy had watched her sister's baptism, she'd watched the minister lower her sister into the water and lift her up again, cleansed. When the red velvet drapes behind the pulpit slid open, you could see only the upper part of their bodies. The drapes framed them like hand puppets.

On the Saturday night before Patsy's baptism, there was a meeting at the church. Carol wasn't allowed to come; Patsy's father said it was not a spectator sport. Patsy and two others, sixteen-year-old Gerald Hall and an older woman who had bought the dry cleaners and was new to the congregation, met the minister in his office in the church basement at seven o'clock and listened while he explained his understanding of the words *decision* and *faith*.

He told them this would be the most important event of their lives. He prayed a short prayer, and after the prayer he read from the New Testament, from Matthew: "And Jesus, when he was baptized, went up straightway out of the water: and, lo, the heavens were opened unto him, and he saw the Spirit of God descending like a dove, and lighting upon him."

They followed the minister, one behind the other, up the winding staircase to the church proper but he stopped on the landing near the top of the stairs and opened a door which Patsy had never seen opened before, exposing a short set of steps, like a stile. He quickly climbed up and then down again into the empty cement tank, and then he turned to offer his hand to whoever was ready to take it.

"Just so you'll have an idea," he said.

The woman who owned the dry cleaners went first. When she got to the top of the steps the minister had to ask her to kick off her pumps, but then she seemed to know what was expected and she jumped down into the tank and stood erect, ready for his arms. When she was finished she went back down the stairs to wait in the office. Gerald said, "I'm last," and the minister leaned out to take Patsy's hand. She was up and in quickly.

The sides of the tank were high, nearly to her chest, and she thought likely there would be room for about six people. There were taps in the corner and a big drain at the bottom and she could smell vinegar. When she asked the minister how high the water would be, he put his hand like a marker about six inches above his belt, smiling, saying he'd never lost anyone. "You just hold your breath," he said. "I'll say a few words and you respond and then I'll lower you." He turned her sideways and took her in his arms. "Okay now," he said. He put one arm around her shoulders and the other hand flat on her chest, as if she had no breasts at all. He tried to force her down but she resisted automatically and lost her balance and she had to stand up straight so he could try again. "Now let yourself go," he said. Gerald watched, leaning on his arms on the rim of the tank.

When she was climbing out, Gerald extended his hands to take her arm. He steadied her down the metal steps and bent to help her put her shoes on. "That's okay," she said. "I can do that."

She went back down the stairs to the office, and when the minister and Gerald were finished they all sat down in a circle again. The minister looked deliberately at each of them and told them that they would soon have a responsibility to witness, to lead others to salvation. He read from Ephesians, "One Lord, one faith, one baptism," and then he prayed another short prayer.

They talked about the order in which they would come upstairs Sunday night and then they were free to go, unless anyone wanted to talk to him privately. Only the woman did. Patsy left quickly. Gerald followed her out the door and, waiting at the curb to be picked up by someone, called out after her, "See you tomorrow night, sinner."

The next afternoon, Patsy met Carol behind the canning factory at the creek, which was full of recent rain and running strong, brown with churned-up mud. They followed it past the end of the town out into the country, something they'd done often when they were eight and nine. Where the creek turned north through the fields of white beans and fence-high corn, they climbed up onto the gravel road, and when the walking got easy Carol tried to take Patsy's arm, the way an adult would. Patsy shook her off. She had been waiting for some kind of Catholic question about the baptism but Carol was aloof and dreamy, savouring the last afternoon of a knowledge which had been unique to her, like a midwife, or a woman of the world strolling the countryside with a virgin.

At the crossroad, where they could turn and walk back into town if they wanted to, Patsy heard someone call her name. Eleanor the blasphemous was out walking too, she stood about a hundred yards down the road that led straight out from town. When Carol saw her, she said, "Turn around, quick," and she hurried back the way they'd come.

Patsy followed her, whispering, "I don't think it would kill us to at least say hi."

"Not today," Carol said. "Any other day, but not today." Without moving her head, Patsy watched Eleanor carry on down the road. Finally she lifted her arm and waved.

"Oh, great," Carol said. But Eleanor didn't respond. She

didn't lift her own arm in a mad reciprocal wave and run to catch them. They were safe.

When they got back down to the creek, Patsy asked Carol if she had her rosary with her. Carol said yes, she always had it, and she carefully pulled a Kleenex from the pocket of her shorts, stopping and opening the Kleenex and holding her hand very still so Patsy could look. It was like a necklace. The dark blue beads were made of cut glass and they absorbed the light from the sun the way jewels would. They were arranged in little groups, with small chains, spaces separating them. The pewter cross dangled on its own short chain and nailed to the cross a tiny twisted Christ with a bowed head died for the sins of mankind.

When Patsy made a grab for the rosary, Carol pulled her hand back but she was too late, Patsy was faster, she untangled the rosary and dropped it over her own Baptist head. She broke into a run along the creek bank, jumping when she had to over the exposed roots of maple trees and random garbage: bike tires, a grey boot, thin coiled strips of rusty metal. The rosary flew around as she jumped and the cross bumped hard against her chest.

Carol had to cry and yell things to try to get it back, things like, "That's mine," and "You're not allowed to touch that," and, finally, loudly, something she didn't really mean, "I hate you." This stopped Patsy. She turned around. She said, "No one's ever going to have to tell you to go to Hell, you know. Because that's where you're going anyway unless you get baptized the way Jesus did." She lifted the rosary from her head and held it bunched up tight in the palm of her hand. She said, "This won't save you. This is just jewellery." She threw the rosary down into the weeds behind her and took off again, running, knowing there was no possibility of forgiveness. She didn't stop to wait or hope for it.

At dinner Patsy's parents and older sisters avoided any talk about what was going to happen that night; there was only a quick checklist of dresses and shoes spoken aloud by her mother with everyone nodding yes, everything was hanging up, everything was fine. Her father got his suit on and drove her over to the church a half-hour before the service was to begin, and when he dropped her off at the Sunday school door he told her not to worry, that this would be just like a lot of other things you only have to do once.

In the choir room, the older woman who had bought the dry cleaners told Patsy she could call her Jessica. They hung their dresses and their slips in the cupboard and put the bags that held their extra bras and panties discreetly on the shelf with the choir hats and chose their crimson gowns. Patsy watched Jessica fold her garter belt with her stockings and tuck them into her shoes and did the same. Above them, the congregation was quietly singing some of the older hymns. Gerald had changed in the minister's office, and when he was ready he came out to sit with them and wait. His feet were huge and white and awkward below his gown and Patsy couldn't help but notice the way the dark hair on his legs stopped abruptly at his ankles and curled. He was to go first. It wasn't long before the minister's wife came down the stairs to get him.

After Gerald left, Jessica stood up and walked around a bit. She blew her nose on a small linen hanky and said to Patsy, "I hope you're not scared. Don't be scared. There's nothing much to it." She got a cigarette from her purse and lit it. She took several deep drags and then dug around for a small silver ashtray with a flip-up lid and put the cigarette out. She said, "You won't say anything, will you."

Patsy said no, she wouldn't.

When the minister's wife brought Gerald back, he had a towel over his head and the choir gown stuck to his back and legs. It dripped a trail as he hurried across the room to the office. The minister's wife sniffed briefly at the air, smiled flatly at Patsy and crooked her finger. Jessica took Patsy's hand, gave it a little squeeze.

At the top of the stairs there was a pile of worn towels waiting and, beyond the stile, the minister. He stood in the tank facing the congregation, holding his open Bible in both hands. He was talking about her, about her decision. He wore one of the men's choir gowns over a white dress shirt and tie and the water was clear, she could see down through it, she could see his gown drifting out around a pair of hip waders. When he finished talking he closed the Bible, setting it on the edge of the tank, and pulled hard on the cord that closed the drapes. He turned to offer his hand to Patsy and she was up and over and in. The water was warm, like secondhand bathwater, and hard to walk through. The choir gown was quickly heavy and she was clumsy as she turned, but he pulled gently on her sleeve until she stood where she was supposed to stand. He winked at her and put his arm around her shoulders, much more forcefully than he had the night before, and he took both of her hands in his and folded them against her chest. Then he reached and opened the drapes with one smooth pull on the cord.

Patsy didn't look out at the congregation. She braced herself, gripped the flat cement floor of the tank with her feet. The minister said all three of her names loudly, like an announcement, and asked did she take Jesus Christ as her own personal saviour. She closed her eyes and he waited and then he leaned his mouth down close to her face. "Patsy," he said, quietly, not quite angry, "you must be sure."

"Go ahead," she said. The organist, who was the only person within earshot and a good friend of Patsy's mother, struck the first chords of "Just As I Am," and the congregation rose and started to sing. The music was soft, reverential.

Patsy closed her eyes and mouth tight against the water. She recognized a slight hesitation in the minister's large hands when she let herself go.

She wasn't under long. But there was time to put to memory both the strength of his arm around her shoulders and the blunt force of his hand on her chest, there was time to feel the pull of the waterlogged weight of the gown and to reach up and take the front of his shirt in her fist.

He didn't flinch. He didn't respond in any way at all. He held her as he'd said he would, just below the surface. The congregation sang on, she could hear them through the water pleading on her behalf as they had pleaded for each other, their words familiar and distinct, and faint, as if from some distance.

For the briefest second she tried to picture the promised Spirit of God, knowing as she tried that the Spirit of God would not descend like a dove, would never, in fact, light anywhere near Patsy Flater. And then she burst up into the air, her mouth wide open to receive it. She didn't have to look down. Her blind bare foot found the bottom step on its own.

DEER HEART

The embossed invitation to lunch with the visiting Queen hadn't come as a big surprise. At forty-one, she found herself included on some far-off protocol list, the result of serving on a minor provincial board or two, the result of middle age.

She wouldn't have made the trip on her own; two hundred miles across the prairie, it wasn't worth it. She'd read the invitation immediately as a chance to be with her daughter, not the Queen, to be off with her on a long drive in the car, contained, remote, private. When she'd asked her daughter to join her at the luncheon the girl had turned down her stereo, briefly, and said, "What Queen?"

She was aware of orchestrating these spaces in time with each of the kids, she'd been doing it religiously since their father's departure. She would have named it instinct rather than wisdom. And they were good, the kids were fine; there was no bed-wetting, no nail chewing, there were no night-mares, at least none severe enough to throw them from their beds and send them to her own in a cold sweat. If they did have nightmares, the quiet kind, they were still able to stand up in the morning with a smile, forgetful.

Her own acceptance, after nearly two years, took an unex-pected form. She'd started files. One file contained the actual separation agreement, which listed all five of their names in full capitals, in bold type, the format generic and formal, appli-cable to any family; with the agreement she kept her list of the modest assets, the things that had to be valued against the day of final division. Another file held the information supplied by her government, little booklets on this aspect of family break-down, supportive statistics on that. And the notification that she would be taxed differently, now that she was alone. In the third file she kept the letters. It was the thickest of the three, although its growth had slowed.

When the mailman began to leave these letters, casually tucked in with the usual bills and junk, she'd been dumb-founded. She'd sat on the couch with her morning coffee after the kids had gone to school, unsealing, unfolding, reading one word after another, recognizing the intent of the words as they arranged themselves into paragraphs of affection. A few of the letters contained almost honourable confessions of steamy fantasies, which apparently had been alive in the world for years, right under her nose. The words *fond of* and *hesitate* appeared more than once.

These men were in her circle, there was no reason to expect they would ever leave it. And they were, to a man, firmly and comfortably attached to women they would be wise to choose all over again, in spite of waists and enthusiasms as thick and diminished as her own. She disallowed all but one of the fantasies with laughter and common sense and a profound appreciation for the nerve behind the confessions.

Her short-lived defence, the time she gave in, had been what she called her net-gain theory. She tried to explain that any increased contentment for her would have to mean an equivalent loss for some other woman. She said that nothing new would be created. She said it was like chemistry. Her admirer had stood with his hands on her hips and told her it wasn't her job to measure and distribute; he'd told her to relax, to lighten up. And she did lighten up, for about an hour.

She kept the letters. If she was hit by a truck on the way to the Tom Boy, she would simply have to count on whoever went through her things to take care of them. The fireplace was just a few feet from her desk.

Her husband, her ex-husband, had found acceptable companionship, young companionship, young smooth-skinned fertile companionship, much more readily. A different life altogether.

When the big day came, she and the girl began the drive to the small prairie city where the Queen was to lunch with her subjects as she'd hoped, like an excursion. They stopped for gas and jujubes and two cans of Five Alive. They talked about school and the broad wheatland through which they were moving. She pointed out how bone dry it all was, told the girl how rain could change the colour of the landscape and how this in turn could change the economy of the province. She told her a little about the people who had to make a living from the parched land, most of the details only imagined. And she told her that when she was twelve she'd kept several scrap-books with Queen Elizabeth II emblazoned on the cover, had filled them with this woman's life, her marriage and corona-tion, the magnificent christening gowns worn by her children, her scrappy younger sister, in love. She confessed all her young need for romance.

Then, without deliberation, she confessed how easily the romance had given way to tacky glamour, the Everly Brothers, James Dean, Brenda Lee. And how easily the glamour had been overtaken by Lightfoot, and Joni Mitchell, and Dylan. She tried to explain Dylan, what she'd absorbed from him, how he'd turned abstractions into something more useful, but without much success. She didn't confess to the next phase, the disdain, although she'd been happy to discover it at the time. She'd used it, while it lasted, without restraint. From this distance, of course, her young, mindless condescension looked merely cramped, and suspiciously safe. It looked like ordinary cowardice.

The girl took it all in, polite in the extreme, and asked the right questions, to please her. And then they were silent, cosy in the car, and she set the cruise control and began to dream a little. She was interrupted by some of the questions she hoped might find their opportunity on this drive. There was a boy. Of course there was a boy.

"Why can't he talk to me normally? I haven't changed," and "Why does he have to sneak looks at me all of a sudden?"

Old questions, easy to answer. She simply told the truth as she knew it, said the words out loud: *longing, confusion, afraid, dream*. She named the feeling a crush and said it was as common as house dust, which made the girl groan and giggle.

And then the girl asked, "Were you pretty?"

"For a time," she said, firmly. Shared, intimate laughter, women's laughter, the first between them. Her daughter's face open and soft.

When they arrived they had only to find the arena and it wasn't difficult. The city was more or less deserted except for the arena parking lot and the streets leading into it. She guessed maybe a couple of thousand people would be involved in this little affair. She parked the car and they cut across the parched, leaf-covered baseball diamond to the arena. Inside they found the washroom and freshened up together, the girl imitating her mother's moves, although with her own style. At the entrance to the huge high-beamed room, which would in a month or perhaps even sooner be transformed into a hockey rink, she found the invitation in her bag and handed it to a uniformed woman.

They waited only a few moments at their seats at the long table and then the orchestra, from the area of the penalty box, began "God Save the Queen." They stood up and in she came. In a hot pink wool coat and a trim little hot pink hat, visible to all, waving and nodding with a fixed, flat smile.

She regretted not wearing what she'd wanted to wear, her cherry red coat and her mother's fox stole, which she'd claimed and kept wrapped in tissue in a closet, an absurdity now with its cold glassy nose and the hooks sewn into the paws. She had no idea why she loved it and longed to wear it, somewhere, before she grew old. She had her mother's opal ring, which she sometimes wore, so it wasn't that, it wasn't just the need to keep her mother's things alive. There was a prayer, for the Queen, for the country, for rain, and then the heavy noise of two thousand chairs being scraped over the cold cement floor. Prairie people, in expensive suits and silk dresses and elegant felt hats sitting down to eat a roast beef dinner for lunch.

She talked superficially and politely to the people around them at their table, people she knew she would never see again, and her daughter listened and tried a couple of superficial lines of her own. "Have you been looking forward to seeing the Queen?" she asked the elderly woman across from her.

They didn't get to shake hands with the Royals, which was an obvious and unexpected disappointment for the girl, but they heard the Queen speak, crisply, about the settling of this land, about the native peoples, textbook talk. She was followed by government officials, unable to resist a go at the captive audience. And then the program began, children in coy little dance groups and choirs and a youth orchestra, and she could feel her daughter wanting to be up there on the stage, performing, taking the only chance she'd likely ever have to curtsy to someone. She wanted to tell her that there had never been anyone who'd made her want to curtsy. She often caught herself wanting to hand over fully developed attitudes, to save the girl time, and trouble.

A couple of hours later, when it was finally over, they were both more than ready to stand up from their hard chairs and leave the arena. After they crossed the ball field with hundreds of other subjects, and found the car, they decided to drive around the city a bit, explore, and, to the girl's way of thinking, they got lucky. There was a shopping mall, brand spanking new. They wandered together through a maze of sale signs and racks of last year's fashions and temporary counters filled with junk jewellery, where they found two pairs of gaudy, oversized, dirt-cheap earrings. The girl did not ask why you never saw tiaras in jewellery stores, which was something she had wondered herself when she was young. The prom queen, not her, not even a friend, had worn a tiara, so they must have been available then, somewhere. Neither of them was hungry, they'd eaten everything served to them at the arena, including magnificent pumpkin tarts, but they sat down to a shared Diet Coke and watched everyone else who'd been at the luncheon wander around the mall. Then it was nearly five o'clock and she said they should get on the road. The girl had school in the morning, and the sitter might be getting worn down.

As they crossed the parking lot she said, "She looks so fat on TV. But she's really not all that fat." The girl laughed in complicity.

In the car, on a whim, because she wanted the day to hold more than the Queen, she dug out the road map and found the big dam, asked the girl if she was interested. "Sure," she said. "Why not?" She told her that they would have to take smaller, older roads to see it and that it might take a little longer going home than coming, if they decided to venture off.

She was glad the girl was game, capable of handling all this distance between their position here in the east central part of this huge province and home. She knew next to nothing about the dam, but she'd seen lots of others and she could improvise if she had to. They could get some books on it when they got home. There might even be a school project on it some day.

It would take about an hour to get near it and then some determining which side roads to choose to get right up to the thing. She drove easily, there was no traffic left for the old highway, not with the dead-straight four-lane fifty miles to the west. She confidently anticipated the curves and set the cruise control again, relaxed. They cut through farmland and then into bush, far more bush than she'd ever seen in this province. The prairie ceased to be open and she began to wonder if making this side trip was wise. The sun that remained was behind the trees, blocked, and dusk, she knew, would be brief. She put the headlights on. There had been a time when she loved being in the car in the dark, like a space traveller, someone chosen, the blue-white dash lights crucial, reliable, contributing precise information, the darkness around her body a release. Some of her best moments had been in dark cars.

The girl was quiet beside her, thinking. About the Queen? About her new earrings, which pair she would allow her sister to borrow if she promised not to leave them somewhere, or trade with a friend? About the boy who could no longer talk to her, normally?

The deer appeared in the corner of her eye. It had every chance. It was thirty yards ahead of them, in the other lane. All it had to do was freeze. Or dive straight ahead, or veer left. Lots of choices. She threw her arm hard across her daughter's chest, forgetting that she was belted in, and she kept her steering as steady as she could with the grip of one firm hand. She braked deliberately, repeatedly; she did not slam the pedal to the floor. She locked her jaw. Just hold tight, she told the deer. Just close your eyes and hold tight. When it dove for the headlights she yelled "Shit," and brought her arm away from the girl's chest back to the wheel. And then it was over. She'd hit it.

Before she could say, Don't look, the girl did. "I think you took its leg off," she said. "Why didn't you stop? Why did you have to hit it?"

She saw again the right headlight coming into sudden, silent, irrevocable contact with the tawny hindquarter. The thump belonged to something else, seemed to come neither from the car nor from the deer.

"You killed a deer," the girl said.

She pulled the car over to the side of the dark road and they sat there, waiting for her to do something. She put her hand on the door handle and unbuckled but she made no further move. Wherever it was, it was beyond her help. Her daughter looked back again.

"He's in the ditch. I think he's trying to climb out of the ditch."

"I'm sorry," she said. "I couldn't go off the road to save him. We'd be the ones in the ditch if I'd tried. I'm really sorry."

She pulled slowly back onto the road and, remembering her

seat belt, buckled up. She took note of the reading on the odometer.

"Are we just going to go?" the girl asked.

"I'll have to find someone to kill it," she said. "We'll stop in the next town. That's all there is to do. I don't feel really good about this either."

The girl sat in silence, pushed down into her seat.

Ten minutes later there was a town, a small group of houses clustered around one long main street, the only sign of life at the Sands Hotel. She pulled in and parked beside a blue half-ton.

"I'll just go in and talk to someone," she said. "You might as well wait here. It won't take long."

She got out and walked to the front of the car. The fog lamp had been bent like a walleye and the glass on the headlight was broken but there was no blood. She'd broken bones, not skin. She noticed for the first time a symbol on the Volvo's grille, the Greek symbol for the male, the circle with the arrow pointing off northeast. She remembered the first time she'd seen it, when she was a girl watching "Ben Casey" on television, wholeheartedly in love with him, with his dark face and his big arms, a precursor to the men she would really love, later. And now it was later than later, and here she was in a bleak prairie town with grey hair growing out of her head, an angry adolescent in her car and a mangled deer twelve kilometres behind her on the road.

Inside the hotel she went directly to the young blond bartender to explain what she'd done, but she'd known the instant she was in the bar which of them would be the one to go back and find the deer and finish it off. They were sitting in a large group around a table, watching her, eight or ten of them in green and brown and plaid, drinking beer and coffee. She knew she looked ridiculous to them in her high black boots and her long dark trenchcoat with the oversized shoulders, like something out of a bad war movie. Still, they waited in well-mannered silence for her to speak.

"Talk to him," the kid at the bar said, pointing. She approached the table and a couple of them, the older ones, tipped their hats. One of these hat-tippers leaned back in his chair and asked, "Pussycat, pussycat, where have you been?" and it took her a few stalled seconds to reply, "I've been to London to visit the Queen." He chuckled and saluted her with his coffee.

"I've hit a deer," she said. "About twelve kilometres back. I was wondering if someone could maybe take care of it." She looked at the one she'd picked.

"North?" he asked.

"Yes," she said. "On number ten."

"How bad?" he asked.

"I think I pretty well ruined his hindquarters," she said.

"Your car," he said. "I meant your car." There was no laughter.

"The car's all right," she said. "My insurance will likely cover it."

"You should report it," he said. "You have to phone the wildlife people. Unless you want to pay the two-hundred deductible. You call and report it now, it's the deer's fault."

"Is there a phone I could use?" she asked.

He led her out of the bar into a cold back room. The light was amber, muted, dusty. There was a stained sink in the corner and a battered leather couch along one wall, the rest of the room was filled with beer cases, stacked four high. There was a pay phone, and beside it, taped to the door-frame, a list of phone numbers. He put his own quarter in and dialled the number for her.

She took the phone and talked to a woman at an answering service who put her through to a man who was in some way official and she gave him all the information she could, the time and location, her registration and licence numbers, her apologies. She couldn't tell him how old the deer might have been.

While she stood there, reporting the incident, the man stayed on the arm of the couch, watching her. She became aware of her perfume and her long, wild hair.

When she was finished he got up and stood beside her.

"Someone hits a deer here about once a week," he said. He reached behind her head and turned down the collar of her trenchcoat, slowly. She would not have been surprised if his mouth had grazed her forehead. "I can check your car."

"The car's okay," she said. "The engine didn't take any damage."

"Whatever," he said.

"My daughter's out there," she said. "She's pretty upset."

He nodded. "This kind of thing is hard on kids."

Outside, he hunched down in the light from the hotel sign and ran his hand over the shattered glass. "Looks like it was a young deer," he said, standing up, stretching. He opened the car door for her and she climbed in behind the wheel. "I've got my gun in the truck," he said. "I'll go back for it."

"Thank you," she said.

He tucked her coat around her legs and closed the door.

On the highway again, the girl listened to the explanation of the procedure. She sat in silence for a long time, her legs under her on the seat, trying, in spite of the seat belt, to curl up. When her mother turned on the radio, to some easy listening music, she started in.

"I don't see why she has to be there every weekend we go to Dad's," the girl said. "I don't see why we have to see her lying in bed in the morning. I think it's rude."

"Where did this come from?" she asked. But she knew the answer. It came from a very young woman riding in a dark car through the bush with her mother.

"You could tell your Dad if it bothers you, her being there when you are. Or I could, if you want me to."

"I already have," the girl said. "He just tells her. They don't care."

"Your Dad cares," she said. "He's not himself. But he misses you. He's told me and I believe him."

"She bought that nightshirt I wanted, the mauve one," she said. "She bought it for herself. And she doesn't get dressed till lunchtime." She reached for the radio and punched in a rock station. "She's everywhere you look."

"That's why you changed your mind about the nightshirt?" she asked.

There was no answer.

The young lady in question had not shown any particular skill at the unenviable task of winning the affections of a middle-aged man's half-grown kids. Although she'd tried. One weekend she'd even done their wash, an effort to appease the mother who bitched about sending them off clean and getting them back, always, in disorder. When they got home they'd stood in the kitchen emptying their weekend bags, showing off their clean clothes. In her pile, the girl discovered pink bikini panties not her own. She tossed them hard across the room to her sister, who screeched and pitched them like a live hand grenade to her defenceless brother, who cringed and ducked.

"She loves your Dad," she said.

"Because you won't," the girl said.

"I'll talk to him," she offered.

"Don't bother," the girl said. "I'll just get a lecture about how everyone's got a right to be happy and all that crap."

"It's not crap," she said.

She wanted to be his wife again, just for a little while. She wanted to talk to him about what people, very young people, have a right to. She'd heard more than once, from her friends, from the inarticulate counsellor, from a British homemakers' magazine in her doctor's office, the theory that kids could withstand a lot. All you had to do was look around you, all these kids carrying right on. She bought into it herself, sometimes, taking pride in their hard-won stability, their distracted smiles. Good little pluggers, all.

The girl stared out her window, watching the bush fly by. "Don't ever expect me to say good morning to some boyfriend of yours."

"No," she said. "I won't be expecting that."

They drove on. She could think of nothing light and harmless to say, nothing would come.

"I saw this TV show," she said, hesitating.

The girl waited.

"There was a woman standing in front of a mirror and she was very unhappy. It was just a dumb mini-series. Anyway, she was standing talking into this mirror, to someone behind her, and she said when she was a kid she'd been driving with her father in a car, at night, like we are, and it was winter, there was a lot of snow. And they saw a deer draped over a fence. It looked dead. She said she began to cry and her father told her it was all right. He told her that deer have a trick. When they're trapped like that they don't have to wait to die. They can make their hearts explode."

"A trick," the girl said.

"I think it would be fright," she said. "I think it would be a heart attack brought on by fright. That would be the real explanation. But it means that our deer could be out of its misery before that man even gets to it with his gun. It could have been dead before we left it."

Even as she recited this she knew it was unlikely. She assumed the deer was back there, not far from the ditch, dying the hard way. It would watch him approach, hear the soft "Easy now. Easy."

And she knew that one of them would hold the deer forever in her mind, not dying, but fully alive in the bright shock of the headlights, and that the other would hold it just as long cold and wide-eyed, after the hunter.

NIPPLE MAN

John McLarty's furniture, in his office in the History Building, his old teak desk and the two extra chairs and the filing cabinets and the bookshelves and the potted plants, had been rearranged over the years into every conceivable configuration. And he'd replaced the drapes, at his own expense, twice. He believed there was a perfect arrangement, something conducive to clear thought and to an overall peace of mind for himself and everyone who entered his office. He'd had some help, initially from his reluctant wife, and then from two or three of the others, and recently even his daughter had spared him a Sunday afternoon. They'd shared a bottle of wine as they hauled things around and argued amicably about what looked best where.

His window, which he liked directly in front of him when he sat at his desk, overlooked the largest expanse of grass left on the campus since the building program of the seventies. The grass, a dozen shades of green on any day of the week from April through October, was usually spotted with the small bodies of students wandering purposefully from one lecture to another. A narrow sidewalk connected John's building to Talbot, farther up the hill, where the economics people plied their trade. He'd never been there. Seventeen years on this campus and he'd never even thought to walk over. Everything he needed was on his own floor and the floors beneath him: colleagues, support staff, archives. He did, of course, use the main library at the base of the hill, but none of the other faculties overlapped his own. Except socially, for those who could endure it. He wasn't one of those who could endure it.

They'd given their share of dinner parties when they'd first arrived, or Carol had, he'd simply been there to pour the Scotch, and they'd continued for a few years to make appearances at the gatherings orchestrated by his fellows in the history department. And then they'd eased out. Carol had eased them out. She'd said, one spring evening, standing in her panty hose and camisole at the bathroom mirror applying her blush, sucking in her tummy, that she couldn't go. He thought she might be sick, or premenstrual, or maybe just exhausted from the kids, who were all at the age when they had to be lifted and carried and fed and buckled up and wiped clean and tucked in, but she said no, she was fine, everybody else was sick. And she paraphrased some of the dirty, cynical gossip she'd heard exchanged by warm little groups in kitchens, and she told him about the clammy hands tracing her rear end when they were crowded around pianos in living rooms, supposedly singing, and about the rigorous, nerve-racking effort needed to keep the whole thing in perspective. And the clincher, which had been a whispered longing expressed in their own backyard by a dull-witted Yank, who had long since departed for greener academic pastures, to see her nipples. She said she'd wanted to strip off her blouse and bra right there at the barbecue and say, There you go darlin', and aren't they as plain as plain can be, and you will notice they are not erect under your gaze and there's not a snow-ball's chance in hell they ever will be, and now will you please just pass me that jar of mustard.

John was astonished, but he knew better than to accuse her of exaggeration. The thought occurred to him that maybe she wasn't exaggerating at all. "You didn't say that," he said, plugging in his shaver. "What did you really say?" "Nothing," she said. "I said nothing. Nothing at all. I walked over to you and Jenny and interrupted some inane discussion you were having about a cactus."

They'd skipped the dinner party. They'd gone instead to a dismal Bergman film and seen Liv Ullmann's nipples, which, if he remembered correctly, and he did, were not as plain as plain can be. That night, after the film and the coffee and the talk about everything but the film, when they climbed into bed, when he should have been his most attentive, he fell sound asleep and dreamed. And from that night his dreams began, habitually, to welcome other women. He couldn't remember dreaming about other women before, not habitually.

The marriage lasted only four more fretful years and then off she'd gone with the kids and her nipples and most of the best family photographs. She'd finished her stalled degree at John's expense, tit for tat, she'd said, at another university and began teaching computer science. She was a respected member of one of the hottest faculties in the country, or so their old friends told him, whenever they could work it in. And she'd married a moderately successful architect. They lived with the kids who were still at home in a house overlooking the Pacific, which they'd built on a great slab of smooth brown rock. John had been welcomed there often, for the sake of the children. He'd never once manoeuvred the preposterous slope of the driveway without feeling like an impotent uncle, but he'd endured, he'd wanted to hold his kids as they grew. And everyone understood. There were lots of books on this kind of stuff.

For a time, he'd attributed their marital disaster to the dull-witted Yank at the barbecue, but then he'd relented and acknowledged the debilitating habits, many of them his own, and the hard knots of temperament that appeared and reappeared like rocks thrown up by a field. On really good days he was content simply that they'd made it as far as they had, and that the damage, if his accounting could be trusted, had been minimal. He'd never told her what he dreamed of, habitually, only that he dreamed. And she'd had the decency to keep the worst of her secrets to herself. He had watched her keeping them.

He'd sold the house; he had no interest whatsoever in screwing her around financially, although his lawyer indicated, with some enthusiasm, that it could be done. She'd worked as hard as he'd worked and what she had with the kids wasn't exactly tenure. And no one else really knew or cared how great the kids were turning out, no one else knew or cared that she'd laughed them all through more than one rough spot.

He'd found an apartment and was no sooner into it and lonely than they started to show up in his office, the women from his dreams, with their nipples. Not the exact women, but very close. In retrospect, those years, seven or eight of them, would run in his mind like a long raunchy film, one naked young body following another. Not that they weren't fine women, some of them. Occasionally, more than occasionally, he remembered their fineness.

Most of them were simply young. They didn't talk in sentences. They wouldn't eat anything, wouldn't cook or sit still to eat a decent dinner. They wore T-shirts and only T-shirts with their jeans. And they expected him to make love to them with a wisdom he couldn't count on all night long and half the next day. They were enthralled by nakedness and long stretches of time and their own capacity to enjoy skin and nerve endings and they lied to him about his virility, not huge lies, but lies just the same, and necessary.

They installed in him a status which was false, although flattering beyond anything he'd ever known. They looked up to him, literally, with sweet smooth cheeks.

He consoled himself with the conviction that he'd freed them all to go after what they wanted, and most of them did. Some had returned to his office boasting degrees better than his own and two had come back to show off babes in arms and fuller hips and breasts relaxed into a new purpose. Given the chance, he would have carefully set the infants on the floor beside his filing cabinets to nap inside their downy sleepers while he jumped their still familiar mothers.

The victorious visits had more or less stopped when he found Marion. He was marching alone down the library steps one balmy Indian summer evening, gazing up through the trees, and he might actually have fallen over her if she hadn't spoken. "Careful," she'd said, and he'd excused himself, feeling clumsy, certainly potentially clumsy. She sat near the bottom of the long flight with eight or ten books piled beside her on the step, exposed by one of the high new lights installed for campus security. He noticed immediately that her cheeks were wet. She wasn't young. A young woman in tears on the library steps would not have slowed him down.

He assumed that a public display from a woman this age did not indicate anything personal, he guessed she was in some kind of physical discomfort, that she'd been hurt, and he was right. She said she was just back to work and was likely pushing it too hard but she was so damned tired of waiting to feel herself again. She said she supposed she should get the books back inside and then go home and watch David Letterman or something. He told her he didn't see that such drastic action was necessary, and he began to load her books, economics texts, two geography, one Welty and one Hardy, into his briefcase and then into his arms.

"Can you stand?" he asked. "My car is just over in the north lot. I'll bring it around and then I'll take you home." And he hauled her books across the cool grass to the north lot. It didn't occur to him until he was back and helping her into his car to ask her who she was. She said she was Marion Alderson; she taught economics, had done so for three years on this campus and for many other years on other campuses across the country. Maid Marion he'd called her and she'd raised her eyebrows, smiling only slightly. She said she was just getting over a little bit of surgery and that she lived in one of the high rises on the other side of the bridge. After he got her home, up the elevator and into her suite with her books settled on an elegant glass desk in her living room, he saw, when her back was turned, that she had a set of those perfect calves that actresses from the fifties used to have, with heavier thighs, he could read them under her dress as she walked. He accepted her graceful thanks and took his leave, feeling a little bit the hero, feeling decent and light on his feet.

He didn't phone her, didn't even think of phoning her until one cold morning two months later when he was marking a particularly fine paper on the Boer War. He found his directory and there she was, name, rank and telephone number. He told her he wanted to know only if she was feeling herself yet and she said yes she was and thanks again for the gallant assistance, and when he didn't take the conversation to its natural close she asked if she could buy him lunch in the Talbot faculty dining room as a token of her gratitude. Sure she could, he said.

So they met, properly, surrounded by economics people he recognized but didn't know. And she was much better, much stronger. She wore an expensive shirtwaist, paisley, Carol had wanted such dresses when they couldn't afford them, and very fine leather shoes with narrow high heels. The shoes, he knew, were worn to show off the legs. Her hair looked especially clean and full, it was a dark grey blonde and it swayed around her head as she talked. Only her eyes, a guarded deep brown set off by rays of crow's-feet, disappointed him. As he ate his grilled cheese he imagined them unguarded and bright, throwing off a phrase or two from the accumulated vocabulary of experienced eyes.

Now that she was well, her voice was clipped and business-like and funny. She was one of those women who wear no rings but talk without apology about their grown-up children. Her breasts seemed full and solid although he couldn't begin to find her nipples; they were lost beneath the swirling blue paisley. After two hours they counted between them, with some guilt, five students left waiting in the halls outside their offices.

He liked her, he decided he liked her tremendously, and by the time the woman came to clear their plates he felt a potent urge to be in love again. As he walked back across the grass to his office he very deliberately resurrected everything he knew to be true and ridiculous and daunting about this urge. He lined it all up, chose what he wanted to believe, and dumped the rest into the bunkers long since dug at the back of his brain. He was going to get into her pants and he was going to fall in love, in whichever order was necessary. She could decide the order.

It didn't take him long to fall in love. She was available and game. They went to concerts in the city park put on by a youth orchestra and to a fall fair thirty miles out of the city and once to the horse races, where he lost forty dollars and she came away even, and smug. They talked about her ex-husband and about Carol over Caesar salad and beer, and about books she'd had a chance to read that year and about recent economic theories he'd wanted to comprehend. And she said one evening, while putting down a twenty for her part of the dinner, that she had no credit cards. She said she thought unnecessary debt was very unwise. That night he'd stood in his kitchen in his boxers and cut his Visa card into pieces with his nail scissors. The next day he transferred enough money out of his savings account to pay off every cent owed to everyone for everything.

They even had a short Sunday afternoon at her apartment with two of her children and one of his own, all gathered in the city for their own youthful, compelling reasons. The young visitors eyed each other tenuously as they threw back beer nuts and pretzels and they circled their parents warily, as had been predicted, but they did give brief, spontaneous lip service to companionship and fun, for anyone. The companionship line, full of good cheer, had come from his own long-legged son, gratis. "Just drink your beer," he'd told him.

He expected by this time, quite honourably, he thought, to be into her pants. She was friendly almost beyond bearing, she touched his arm or his back whenever there was even the mildest excuse to do so. But she'd said no twice to his offer to tuck her up and she kissed him chastely.

Because he knew no other way, he asked her flat out one night, over a late dinner after an economics lecture which he'd enjoyed and agreed with, why they weren't making love. "I want to bite those thighs," he said. He didn't broach her nipples; he wasn't entirely without discipline.

She plopped sour cream over her baked potato and loaded it with chives. "I'm forty-seven years old," she said. "I would bet you've never been with a forty-seven-year-old woman."

"No," he said, grinning.

"It's no joke," she said.

He knew what had to be done. He was sure he could match her. He listened to her go on about Dostoyevsky over dessert, and as soon as they were into the car in the parking lot he pulled his shirt out of his pants and let his stomach hang out over his belt, although it wasn't as disgusting in the dark as he'd hoped. He took her hand and placed it on his soft, hairy pot.

"There," he said. "Isn't that nice?"

She took her hand away.

He hiked up his pant leg and pointed to a long lumpy vein just under the skin. He'd been watching its steady movement to the surface for years.

"Look at this," he said. "Like an old log bobbing up."

She watched his excitement calmly for a minute and then she lifted her bum off the seat and pulled her dress up to expose her thighs.

"Yes, indeed," he said. "I'd recognize them anywhere." He started the car and got them on their way, sticking to the passing lane of the main thoroughfare from the city core out to the campus.

"There's more," she said.

He turned off onto a quiet side street, continuing home at a steady fifty kilometres an hour. She had unbuttoned her shirtwaist, this one a soft green print, and was pulling her arms out of it as he drove. He saw, glancing as often as he could in the intermittent light from the street, what she wanted him to see. Her lacy black bra was filled with something other than flesh, something similar in texture and shape to the kids' old beanbags. She reached around and unhooked her bra, letting it fall heavily into her lap. He was looking at a war zone.

He slowed and pulled the car over to the side of the road. As soon as his hands were free he turned and used them to cover the two nearly healed slices. His thumbs moved involuntarily, up and down, up and down, over the rough dark texture.

Her eyes were bright, finally, but not with the sulky passion he'd put there in his dreams. Her smile looked empty, and raw.

"They don't hurt much any more," she said.

He leaned over and buried his face in her. The scars felt tough and final against his cheek, as if the cells had hardened and said, This is it, don't ever cut here again. He was astounded by their warmth, scars as warm as flesh can be.

"You might have told me," he said.

She put her hand into his thinning hair, lifted it between her fingers and let it fall back into itself, soft and orderly. She said, "I'm telling you now."

He could hear her heart as clearly as he'd heard his own when he'd been alone and listening for it. He took what he could into his mouth, the thick layers of tissue where the needle had gathered the skin, the sturdy ridges rising like a mountain chain where all other land had disappeared.

He knew escape was a possibility. There were ways, and he'd had some practice. He could be bravely direct or he could be subtle, clever, cowardly. It wouldn't matter much. She was braced for anything. He could feel her fingers drifting absently through what was left of his hair. She might have been on Mars.

"They're in my mind," he said. He rubbed his cheek against her. "I've got them." He bent down to her thigh, sank his teeth, gently. He took her firm and shapely flesh between his teeth. He could hear the sharp intake of her breath above him and then a sound that might have been laughter, if laughter is sometimes brutal.

JIGGLE FLICKS

The sailboat Heather had been tracking across the bay was small in the distance now, almost gone, so she gave her attention over to the other boats. She counted five moving back in to the shoreline, homing gracefully to the squat, brightly painted boathouses which lined the bay like suburban garages.

She didn't try to imagine the people who sailed the water, their faces given over to laughter or hesitancy or plain brute effort. She didn't wonder what elaborate skills were needed to control the direction and speed of a sailboat, or what kind of nerve it took to sail on a bright western afternoon out of Vancouver Harbour into the Strait of Georgia. Sitting there, holding her seven-dollar glass of Scotch, trying to put to memory the surprising colour of the sun on the water, she thought the most compelling argument for sailing is that it gives people on the shore something magnificent to watch.

She was tired. She'd come down to the lounge from the conference rooms with all the others hoping to unwind, hoping for pleasure or, at the very least, distraction. They'd taken the available tables in a fluid five-table rush and ordered their drinks anxiously, as if thirsty, and as they settled they took care of the first order of business, which was to dismiss the last panel discussion they'd heard as not especially useful or incisive. They always did this. And then the stories began.

Complaints and accomplishments were brought out like baby pictures and passed from one to the other around the tables, the interest expressed sometimes sincere, sometimes not quite. Although they had been together once or twice a year for some time, there was some backtracking to do; people tended to forget what they were supposed to remember. A few pas de deux were under way: a coy or steady glance, devout attention proffered like a gift certificate, a hand on a back, felt, and known to be felt. Married, not married, troubled, trustworthy, pitiful, wild, careless, smart, just about everyone had something to offer. Those who had performed together before were discreet, tolerant of new couplings, ignoring the signs they'd received or sent themselves another time. Insurance people did this, she thought, museum people. Plumbers?

After she'd got her Glenlivet, Heather had turned a deaf ear to the conversation and swivelled her chair an inoffensive half turn to face the windows. There was a full bank of them, from floor to ceiling, overlooking the wide blue bay. Her sightline across the lounge was interrupted only intermittently by the heads and shoulders of the other drinkers and occasionally by deferential waiters in tight rose jackets bending to deliver drinks. She supposed the drinkers seated closest to the windows were regulars, or real tourists who knew enough to flash a bit of money.

Tom was already in up to his ears. Heather had talked to him briefly at the first conference breakfast; he'd told her she looked beautiful, he'd asked about the kids. When they came into the lounge she had stalled and watched to see where he was going to sit and had pulled out a chair at another table, but then he'd moved, following in the wake of a happy young woman who smoked, much to everyone's annoyance. Six feet away, he leaned eagerly forward into the smoke, taking care to catch the young woman's words, prompting her. Tom listened well in the beginning, although what he remembered later, at least in her case, had been a little distorted, the names of cities and towns got wrong, significant people thoughtlessly dismissed. She had tried once or twice to correct him, but she'd waited too long. Things had set in his mind.

The happy young woman who smoked had several spectacular bangles on each arm and she was playing with them, pushing them up to her wrists and letting them slide down her forearms again, explaining their origins, the words Africa and New Mexico carrying through the air more forcefully than some of her other words. Tom reached over and slid one of her bangles off and, laughing, attempted to push it down over his own hand. Heather knew it wouldn't go past his knuckles, and it didn't. She wanted to call over, Take note, sweetie, of those large hands.

Someone had ordered her another Scotch. The waiter was smiling down at her, lifting her empty glass from her hand. She heard talk about dinner. Vietnamese, someone said. She thought she might skip out, an aunt to call, an old friend. But then again. She looked out once more over the water. The formation of the sailboats had changed. The one she'd been tracking was lost entirely and three new ones, recently set sail, drifted close to the shoreline, anxious for the wind. The colours over the bay had deepened, almost imperceptibly.

She turned back to her companions and threw herself wholeheartedly into the middle of a discussion about municipal bylaws. There were seven people around the table. She gave her attention to a quiet, balding man she'd sometimes seen but never talked to, who had never, as far as she knew, shown much interest in her or in any of the others. His name was Jim. She thought perhaps he was deliriously happy with someone none of them had ever heard about. She thought perhaps he was loyal to someone. She wondered if this loyalty signified moral stature or if he'd just had himself some blind luck. It certainly made him worth talking to.

One of the other women at the table, Sheila, from New Brunswick, had begun to talk earnestly about being hungry and so it was arranged that the drinks would soon stop and they would meet in the lobby in half an hour and get cabs to a restaurant on East Hastings. As she was digging in her briefcase for her share of the bill, Heather noticed that the happy young woman who smoked had stood up and was moving to another table to talk to a colleague from Calgary, a too-young corporate lawyer who looked a bit like Donald Sutherland had looked when he was young. When the young woman approached him he wrapped his arm around her waist as if all along he had been simply waiting for her to finish up with the other guy, as if he had waited before for other women and didn't mind at all. Tom looked a tad dejected, but then who wouldn't?

Heather had met Tom three years earlier at a subcommittee meeting in Thunder Bay, when she was still subject to a child-like shame at being so obviously on her own in the world. After an initial, fairly aggressive session in his room, they'd had another, quieter go in hers. Near the end he'd casually wrapped his arms around her and held her with a steady, easy, perfect pressure, and he'd said the word beautiful. And then they'd rented a car and taken off, to Kakabeka Falls. They got a cabin and he hurried away to talk to the management about renting a canoe, he was very excited about getting a canoe.

He soon returned with one, carrying it like a woodsman over his shoulders, grinning. She stood on the dock watching as he lowered it to the shore, pushed it into the water and walked it out along the dock with a paddle. Then he stepped down into it and held it steady for her, his free hand extended. She shook her head. "Thanks anyway," she said.

"I thought you liked the water," he said. "Why don't you like the water?"

"For the same reason fish don't like land," she said.

"You told me your family always went to a lake," he said. "There must have been boats."

"Motorboats," she said. "My brothers skied."

"Ah," he said. "Motorboats. And sunglasses and bikinis and cases of beer and very loud music."

"And convertibles," she said.

"Ontario," he said, chuckling, pushing off. He paddled with some expertise out into the cold northern lake.

She sat at the end of the dock, her legs dangling over the edge, and when she looked down through the water she could see that good-sized rocks had been piled around support posts to hold the dock in place. She could see small dark fish hovering near the rocks, moving as if chased from one crevice to another. A few tangled plants appeared to be rooted to the rocks' smooth surfaces and they drifted with the water's movement, untangling. There was no wind that she could feel and she wondered what made the water move like that, below the surface.

She heard, intermittently, the quick plop of fish, pike, she supposed, coming to the surface for food, and one other sound, surrounding her, composed like orchestral music from dozens of smaller sounds. Some of the insects were in the air above the water, some hovered on the surface, snacks for the pike, but most of them were behind her, tight to the earth or in it. Although she couldn't hear any animal sounds, she assumed there would be several species not very far away, which, if she didn't disturb, she could comfortably ignore.

Tom had moved directly to the centre of the lake and some tension on the surface of the water kept him there. He'd lifted the paddles and was lying back in the canoe, stretched out. On the surrounding shoreline, boulders which had been deposited in half-submerged clusters held the lake in place, reflected the wet light. Substantial trees, mostly spruce and pine, pulled back from the shore and grew dark and thicker in the distance, which was clear enough under the stars. She waved to him, in case he was watching, but he didn't respond. She guessed he was looking at the sky.

From the dock, it appeared perfectly safe out there and she thought she'd likely made a mistake, refusing. She thought perhaps it would be smarter to welcome something new, something never tried, never trusted. There was lots to be replaced, many things she had once done well, often with panache and some grace, that were out of the question now: the long jump, the jive, giving birth, falling in love.

Although she couldn't have put an exact time on it, before her divorce or during or after it, before one miserable, middle-aged cancer death or during or after another, somewhere along the line she'd come to believe that beauty was nothing more than a man-made distraction, an anxious imperative, that much of what was called beautiful was only cruel and raw, barbaric: rocks, for instance, and rivers, the wind-tempered growth of a tree, the black sky and the secluded stars that sometimes seemed to fill it, certainly mountains. Once, shortly after her divorce was finalized, she was sitting alone in her backyard with her face turned up to the sun and a Monarch butterfly took rest on her bare shoulder. She was breathless, amazed, thankful. But it stayed too long, longer than seemed possible, and when she turned her head to look she saw that it had been partially dismembered. It couldn't leave. Through those years she'd never stopped hearing the word *beautiful*, it's a word people frequently say, but she'd come to understand the word the same way she understood the sound of a whip used on a circus lion, as the sound needed to enforce distance, to create an illusion of calm.

Sitting on the dock, watching Tom float at the centre of the lake, surrounded on all sides by the shadows and the sheen, the haphazard, moving patterns, the oblivious confidence of even the mindless pike, she understood the word differently. It bounced off the water like light, like crystal. It was absorbed by the dense growth of trees along the shoreline and re-emerged to hover softly over the drifting canoe. It pushed across the lake toward the dock, toward her, not a trick word at all, just a word like any other, used to describe things which could not be otherwise known.

Later in bed, with her face comfortably tucked into Tom's fleshy shoulder, she could smell the lake still on his skin, she could see with her eyes shut tight the trees and the boulders and the light. When his casual arms enclosed her, with their perfect pressure, as if some dreamed of perfect coupling had been achieved, she tried to tell him how things had looked from the dock.

Sheila stood up and was asking was she coming for dinner, so she finished the last of her drink and followed her through the lobby past the fake statuary to the elevators, resisting the urge to run a hand through her dishevelled hair as they passed the inevitable mirrors. They were joined in the elevator by a young bellman in a grey and rose uniform who carried, at shoulder height, a silver tray of drinks and cocktail food covered by a white cloth. As the elevator rose he slipped his hand under the linen to get a cracker spread with smoked salmon pâté, and when Heather laughed out loud he got one for her too.

At her room, she walked out of her shoes before the door closed behind her and made for the bed, thinking about fresh sheets and room service and the recommended book of stories she'd bought written by a guy named Hodgins, set on Vancouver Island. She dropped onto the bed and curled up on her side, closed her eyes. She wondered briefly if this more than occasional preference for solitude, for the absence of sound, this choosing sometimes only the dimmest of lights, was some kind of gradual backhanded practice for the hereafter, and then she thought she could likely have done without the last Scotch.

Her third conference outfit hung on the closet door. Two down, two to go. It was a floral print dress, long and loose and bright. Stockings the exact shade of the chrysanthemums were in the pocket. Stockings to match the mums, she thought, no one could say you aren't trying. She'd bought the dress in a brief fit of post-divorce confidence, the same week she'd bought an expensive new mattress and decided to have the sofa recovered in chintz. She'd read in the *New Yorker* that divorced women should avoid chintz furniture like the plague and she'd thought, Chintz would be nice. The dress was still good four years later; she was still sure of the dress.

In the shower she remembered home, the kids. When she was away from them they came to her more concretely than when they were in her arms. Some kids they'd made. Worth every fight, every humiliating session with the divorce lawyers and the judges, all the regretful separation tears. Once she had gathered the kids together in the chintz living room and tried to tell them how they filled her. It was a stupid idea. The language she'd needed to use was too rich for them, they resisted mightily, shrugging, saying that they only wanted her to be happy, that they were fine. I know that, she said, that's the whole point, how very fine you are. And then she'd backed off and one of them cracked wise and it was over.

In the dress, in the stockings, she stood at the mirror lifting her hair up and letting it down again. It should be up, she thought and I should be young, and there should be a saucy hat to match the dress, but there isn't, so there you are.

The cab ride to East Hastings was long, detoured through Stanley Park, because everyone wanted to see it again. Sheila rolled her window all the way down and the wet air moved through the cab, lifted hearts. It was dark and the smell of the bay in the air and the lights from the city and the bridge and the moving stream of cars sent Heather into the inevitable Vancouver spin. I'll move here, she thought, I'll live here and drive through this park every night, drive over that bridge, up and down those streets. She never would, she knew, but she let herself play with the details: call a realtor in the morning, find out about high schools, ask a couple of colleagues about possible openings, discreetly.

At the restaurant, there was one long table already set up

for them, it filled half the room, and they moved around it and began to find places. Just as she found a seat there was sudden loud laughter from the other end of the table, and when she looked down she saw the bangled young woman who smoked standing in her own floral print dress, mums and all, waving and grinning, what a coincidence, what a funny thing. The others clearly wanted to enjoy this so she gave it to them, graciously. What the hell, she thought, and then Tom was at her arm, pulling her chair out. She thanked him and they sat down.

She picked up the menu immediately but Tom pushed it down to the table and took her hand, introducing her to another young woman, who sat across from them. Andrea something was her name. Andy, she wanted to be called. She was shy and reticent at first but Tom drew her out and then she had lots to say, and no one stopped her. Those at the table who were older, which was most of them, looked suddenly tired, the meetings, the talking, the wine, but they listened and smiled occasionally, and she wasn't half bad, this one, pretty bright as it turned out. Heather watched Tom wonder if his luck, after all, had held.

The last time she'd been with Tom, in Ottawa, in winter, sitting in an East Indian restaurant eating tandoori chicken, he had steered the conversation deliberately, which was unusual for him, coming finally to his point by inviting her to open up about her ex-husband and any other past loves. She wouldn't do it. That was then, she'd said. This is now. As it turned out his curiosity had been only a courtesy, a chance for reciprocity; he had something he wanted to tell her.

Later, in bed, he began the real telling by saying that he'd turned fifty-five since they'd last been together. Happy Birthday, she said. What should I get you? What do you want? He told her that he'd had a new will drawn up and that he'd lost fifteen pounds, jogging, and she said, Oh, yes you have, of course you have. He told her he'd decided there was enough deterioration in middle age without extra weight to compound the problem and she laughed and said, Don't I know, although weight had never been that much of a problem for her. She did say, I used to have a chicken pox scar as big as a dime on my forehead, and now it's in my eyebrow. She did say, Where do you think it's heading? And when he told her he'd culled his wardrobe and his personal files, filled three bags for the Sally Ann and as many again for the dump, she said, I should do that.

Then he asked did she believe in one true and perfect love. Not any more, she said, but he didn't hear. This was to be a telling, not a talk. She laughed at him, already afraid, and then a fog settled in around her, as thick as the fog in a field of icebergs.

"When I was forty-seven," he said, "there was one perfect woman."

"More than one," she said. "Surely."

"No," he said. "Just one."

She got up to turn on the late news, hoping for war, famine, earthquake, anything, but there was only insipid weather, and it didn't stop him.

"Her hair," he said, "was the colour of coal."

She got back into bed, keeping to her own side, but he rolled over, wrapped his arms around her, held her with his perfect pressure.

"She had a really magnificent back," he said. "Long. And long legs. Although she wasn't very tall standing up."

He threw his leg over hers, the way a twin would in the uterus.

"Could we finish this another time?" she asked.

"She had buttocks like a boy's," he said. "And perfect high breasts, as white as clouds." He traced his palm over her own. "Her waist came in from her hips really sharply, like this." He put his hands in the air just above her face, formed a shape. "And all of it held in the most impeccable skin I've ever seen. Even the soles of her feet were flawless."

"Did you get a chance to look in her mouth?" she asked.

"She had no flaws," he said.

"I'd have to call that bullshit," she said.

"I'm trying to tell you," he said.

Heather knew what her moves were. She should ease herself out of the bed, whisper something that would hold a cutting edge for years, then dress, pack and leave. But she stayed where she was, pissed off at the sheer inconvenience of such a course of action, apparently too dulled in middle age for even a little bit of half-decent theatre.

"There is no one else to tell this to," he said. Soon he dozed off, deeply saddened and apparently exhausted from his telling. She watched the dark hair on his chest rise and fall peacefully beside her.

She propped her pillow up behind her back and looked toward the television, and when she could see again she saw Tina Turner madly gunning an armoured jeep through some kind of desert war zone, sitting at the wheel in a suit of chain mail. Her glossy white hair was high in the wind and wild, but the set of her jaw implied the calm that comes from wit, from skill, and her eyes were clear and focused. She was as beautiful as any woman could hope to be and she was having a fine time gunning the jeep through that desert, hanging on hard, hell-bent. Watching from the bed, Heather wanted, as much as anything she'd ever wanted in her life, to be Tina Turner in that jeep, courageously outrunning a monstrous enemy. Or was she burning up all that energy to save someone else? Not likely.

She threw Tom's leg off and lifted her own leg high into the air above the bed, contemplating the length, the shape, the bulky knee, the tough casing of skin over muscle and fat and blood and bone. When she let it drop down onto the bed, heavily, his large hand reached for her forearm and squeezed.

In the morning, they had breakfast together before she arranged for the cab and left him. When their coffee had been refilled, she said, "Do you know about your hands?"

"What about my hands?" he asked.

"They're too large for the rest of your body," she said. "It's the first thing I noticed about you. As if some chromosome was out of whack when you were just a wee embryo. As if a madman cut them from someone else's arms and attached them to yours." She reached across the table. "I've never looked at your wrists really closely," she said. "There might be marks. Let me check." She tried to take one of his hands in her own but he yanked it away, tucked it under the table.

"This is simpleminded retaliation," he said. He bit the skin from his lower lip as he talked, a habit she'd noticed only once or twice before. "I didn't say you aren't beautiful. Although you're not, not this morning."

He wrote to her later that he didn't think her leaving solved anything, and that he didn't think she was being particularly fair to him. He didn't think her leaving was very original either, or profound. He said he was only trying to understand love and its relationship to beauty, and that he didn't see this as a necessarily despicable undertaking. He said he did love her, he couldn't imagine not loving her.

When the Vietnamese dinner was cleared, and it had been delicious, the best she'd ever had except for the one time in London with her ex-husband, the waiters brought fortune cookies, which were passed around to everyone and opened. Her fortune read, "Your future success will depend on your kindness." Good news, she thought, rolling it up like a spitball and dropping it into the onions she'd left in her bowl. Someone decided the fortunes should be read aloud and beginning with Jim on her left, moving around the table away from her, each person shared his fate. "Much success in words and music," they began, "Avert misunderstanding by calm, poise and balance," "A merry heart maketh a cheerful countenance."

When it got back around to their end of the table, Heather unrolled her soggy bit of paper and licked the sauce from her fingers. She could hear the smile in Tom's voice as he read, with all the effect he could summon, "You will live long and well, beloved by many." This brought hearty laughter, he'd known it would.

Then it was her turn and she read aloud, "Your future success will depend on your kindness." More laughter, first from Tom and then from the others. In Tom's laughter she could hear just an edge of the vicious, as if he'd been waiting with his laughter, not impatient but ready, for a while. And all this time she'd thought at least that part was over.

When she looked up, people were involved again in whatever

conversations they'd left, they were waving pieces of fortune cookie around in the air, breaking and eating them. Tom was leaning across the table talking in a low voice to Andy. Jim nudged her arm and said he didn't think she had anything to worry about, she looked pretty kind to him.

Cabs were called again, and when Tom followed her and climbed in after her with Andy in tow, she took his hand in the dark back seat and drove her thumbnail as deeply as she could into the thick flesh just below his knuckles. He shook her off, his face a quick and honest mask of shock. She checked her nail for blood, disappointed.

"I'm only trying to understand love," she said quietly. "And its relationship to bruises."

"What did you say?" Andy leaned forward, smiling.

They rode back through the park again, Jim and Sheila in the front seat chatting up the cab driver, who gave them all the touristy facts and all the oblique mockery anyone could be expected to absorb. Jim didn't much like the mockery, and after the cab driver said he didn't think they'd like living in Vancouver, Jim slugged him playfully on the shoulder, laughing only slightly.

When they were out of the park approaching the bridge, to include her in a vision of the city lights reflected off the water, Tom put his hand on her knee and shook it, as if to waken her.

In the hotel lobby she walked to the front desk with a question about check-out time to which she already knew the answer, waiting until Tom and Andy had excused themselves before she rejoined the others. Jim and Sheila had decided to go for more drinks. She said she thought she'd pass, and yes, she'd meet them for breakfast at eight-thirty, that sounded fine. Jim shrugged his shoulders and smiled, happy that a decision had been made for him.

The elevator doors were just about closed when a fist, and then a bangled arm, blocked them, forcing them to open again on the lobby. The young woman in the floral dress giggled her way in, followed by the lawyer from Calgary. They were holding hands. "Hello," he said, grinning. "Done for the night?"

He hit a button and then moved to stand unnecessarily close to her and, with no warning, slipped his free hand into the pocket of her dress. He said he loved the dresses. He said it was good to see women wearing clothes that belonged on women again. He said good for her, what the hell, she could still get away with a dress like that, so why not? She pulled his hand out of the pocket and placed it on the delicate shoulder of the happy bangled young woman, who was now enclosed in his other arm. "How very kind," she said. She read the neon indicator, hit a button and got out three floors early.

In her room she took off the dress and hung it in the closet. She thought when she got home she'd offer it to her neighbour, an energetic young woman with four kids and an artist husband. Maybe she could get some use out of it. In the bathroom she

brushed her teeth and pulled her pyjamas on, pitched the stockings into the garbage. She walked out to the television set and
sat down on the carpet in front of it, pulled the off/on switch.
She turned the channels knowing there would be no news, it
was too late, but hoping for a movie. She got lucky. She found
Russia House, with Sean Connery, who had earned, since he'd
allowed himself to age and let his hair go, a very secure spot on
her shortlist. The kids had deduced this small lust through her
video preferences at home and they had teased her without
mercy the first time they'd seen an old James Bond film. And
Bette Midler was on, in something obscure that she'd once half
thought of seeing but missed. The other movies were restricted
and she was offered only samplings. Jiggle flicks, Tom called
them. She tried one of the samples. On the screen, just a few
inches from her hand, a thin young woman panted loudly into
the ear of a man whose dark hair was either very greasy or wet.
He was going at her attentively, with discipline and control and
his eyes wide open, as if she were some kind of machine with a
seized motor. It looked like it would go on for quite a while,
and then it stopped and the screen faded. A message came on
telling her that she should push seven on the control panel on
top of the set if she wished to watch the movie in full, that the
cost would be billed automatically to her room. She found Sean
Connery again. He was playing a reprobate, a drunk who'd
known better times, but he was nonetheless enticing and

Michelle Pfeiffer, who was fated to fall in love with him, was wasting her time resisting. Heather thought it would have been much nicer if Connery had turned up in the jiggle flick. Michelle Pfeiffer could have the guy with the greasy hair.

She went back to the bathroom and brushed her teeth again, and her tongue, trying to get rid of a taste from dinner that had been better the first time around. Standing at the window, she wished she'd agreed to pay the extra for a room overlooking the bay. Below her there were only cars, rows and rows of them, dull and similar.

Suddenly tired, she pulled back the covers of the bed and climbed in, taking the heaviest of the pillows and placing it over her feet, as was her habit. Perhaps because she already knew the plot of *Russia House*, she was nearly out when she heard his knock.

She got up and turned the movie off and walked to the door, peering through the glass in the small security hole. The glass worked like the side mirror on a car, it made his face look more distant than it actually was, and slightly malformed. She opened the door.

"She's heard I'm a bit shallow," he said. He walked past her into the room, but not too far. "She says she's been burned before." She let the door close. "Imagine that," he said. "Burned." He moved tentatively to the chair beside the television and sat down. He put one of his massive hands on the channel changer and turned it all the way around, clunk, clunk, clunk, although the set was dead.

"She was quite lively," Heather said. "Doesn't she believe in quick involvement?" She was parroting the phrase from telephone conversations overheard at home.

"Is there any other kind?" he asked.

She climbed back into the bed. She turned from him and shifted around to find the place she'd made for her body just a little while before. "Did you come to tell me how much it hurts?" she asked.

"She was just good company for the night," he said. "I wasn't really trying." He was taking off his shoes. She heard them drop, one after the other, to the floor. He hated shoes. He would be rubbing his feet now, working his toes. "She's too young to be expected to . . ."

She interrupted him. "Tell me how much it hurts," she said. "And put your shoes on."

"You want me to agonize?" he asked. "You want me to agonize over one sweet young thing who won't have me? Because I'm not cock-of-the-walk any more? Because I no longer have quite enough of whatever it is it takes? That's nothing," he said. "That's life."

She lifted her head from the pillow. "You're so brave," she said.

He extended his hand toward her. "I've got your bruise," he said. "It's small but it's going to be a good deep purple." He smiled.

She smiled back.

"You lie there," he said, "grieving for yourself and for me because you won't accept the way things are. Everyone else has to. You waste all this damned energy resisting what can't be resisted. And for what?" He went on, more gently. "We'll be a long time dead. But we're alive now, and we could have . . ."

"This isn't grief," she said. She turned again, this time onto her stomach. The sheets were still cool and they smelled slightly of something she couldn't name, something close to lemon.

"So it's not grief," he said. "Whatever you want to call it, it's not worth . . ."

She decided if she wasn't asleep before he finished his rant she would pretend to be, she would pretend to be in some other place entirely, beyond avoidance, safe. She willed herself to dream peacefully, conjuring the images that worked: each kid, separately; a dock in a dark Northern Ontario night; the desert. She hoped against hope that in the morning when she woke up he would be gone, gone and grateful for her kindness.

She did fall asleep. Oblivion came and was eventually overtaken by a dream. She stood in the middle of a luxuriant vegetable garden, a neighbour's, which she was supposed to tend during some absence. She surprised herself with knowledge she'd assumed she was without; she was able to recognize and identify each buried vegetable by its tough surface growth, she was able to trap the various bugs which were hidden under the leaves and pinch them off, flick them from her finger. She danced along the vegetables, stepped from row to row, a good neighbour.

Tom watched her sleep. It wasn't what he'd come for. He tried not to think about crawling into the warmth he knew she made, in any bed, or about offering up, just one more time, the conviction of his need. He tried not to think about her arms around him, or her legs. He muttered the word "bitch," once, hardly meaning it. If she heard, she didn't respond.

He settled into the chair and waited, unwitnessed, cold and sharply awake, wondering what earthly goddamned good it did, this celibate watching through the night. Toward daybreak he heard her speak several disjointed words from a very deep sleep. One of the words sounded impossibly like turnip.

Ten Men Respond to an Air-Brushed Photograph of a Nude Woman Chained to a Bull

The photograph was originally an eight-by-ten glossy, taken, developed and held for a time in a file with other similar photographs in the expectation that it could be sold.

The woman in the photograph is a toughened twenty-something. Her long hair is platinum blonde with just a slight growth of dark roots at the skull, and deliberately wild; it surrounds a delicate face reminiscent of Tuesday Weld's when she was young and fresh. Her breasts are wide and bulbous but the rest of her body is quite thin, particularly her arms and her neck. She looks healthy except for the few small bruises on the flesh of her upper arms and thighs.

The young woman is standing in a corral with her back partially turned to a full-sized Black Angus bull. Her hands grip the top board of a rail fence. There's a bit of sparse grass outside the fence, and a few weeds, thistles, but the earth in the corral is muddy grey and barren. The bull is about five feet away from her. He is well groomed but glassy-eyed. His thick tongue hangs from his mouth as if it is finally too heavy to hold in, as if he is extremely thirsty.

The woman and the bull are connected by two sturdy chains which extend from her wrists to a leather collar around the bull's neck. She is implicitly but clearly susceptible to any movement the bull might make. If he takes off, if he is spooked, she'll have to try to keep up. If he charges, she's got the rail fence. She'll have to get over it fast, trust its strength. The expression on her face is one of high excitement; anything can happen.

The photograph has been reproduced in a magazine with very good distribution and surprisingly classy ads.

THE PHOTOGRAPHER who captured the image and sold it to the magazine works freelance and lives alone, for the moment, in a medium-sized city. He's been married, once, and has a daughter in another province. The kid's eleven. His ex-wife wanted her and he was easy, one way or the other. He figures it wouldn't be much of a life for a kid living with him. He's away quite a bit.

Recently, he's been attending night classes in computer science. He thinks that's what the future holds. His ex-wife makes noises about money every time he hears from her, she's got stats on how much money it takes to raise a kid and she reads them to him over the phone, long distance. When she says, "Do you hear what I'm saying to you?" he laughs and says, "It's your dime, talk all you want."

The investment in the camera and the darkroom equipment has paid off. He sells photographs whenever and wherever he can. He takes all kinds: city streets, houses, shopping centres, animals, cars, sports, women. The market's there for nearly anything if you can make the connections, although some are easier to move than others. He sends his ex-wife a hundred bucks here and there, when he can, no questions asked. At Christmas, on a whim, he dropped a red fifty-dollar bill into the clear plastic Salvation Army bucket in the mall where he does most of his browsing. He hangs out in malls a lot, studying the walks and stances and faces and overall physical attitudes of spoiled middle-class teenagers.

He didn't know the blonde at the farm. He didn't know the bull either. A friend of a friend set it up. His friend drove him out to this farm in a rented van and they met the blonde there; she'd driven out with another guy, a manager type, who was quite a bit older. The farmer who owned the bull and the local vet were waiting for them at the house, on the porch. Before they started the shoot they each downed a light beer from a case on the porch step. Money was paid and then the guy who owned the bull disappeared somewhere in his truck.

THE PHOTOGRAPHER's response: I'm pretty happy with it, technically. She was an experienced model. There's a nice play, a nice tension between the coarseness of the bull and the dirt, between the roughness of the rails and the bruises, and her obvious delicacy. The light was nearly perfect. You can see how it works differently on everything it hits.

THE PUBLISHER is in late middle age, works as a team with his wife out of their basement in a small New England town. Their daughter works for them as a part-time secretary, takes the calls from their network of photographers and writers around the U.S. and Canada, does the filing and the billing. Their other kids are grown and gone. He didn't know much about publishing when they started, he has his high school certificate and a diploma in drafting, so over the years he and his wife have taken turns attending conferences and seminars for publishers and small-business operators. They have made many useful contacts with people who have been in the business long enough to know the ropes. It's been a long hard climb from nowhere but they feel they have finally established themselves. They know they're not going to get rich by any means, and they've accepted that. All they really want is a half-decent living.

THE PUBLISHER's response: It's staged, of course. Ninety-nine per cent of this stuff is staged, just like most of what you get at the newsstand, only the rest of it's called journalism. The bull is doped to the gills. The bruises are made up. We've never allowed ourselves to get pulled into the kind of stuff where people can get hurt. There's no need, really. And the girls get paid, more than you'd think, likely more than you and I get paid. That particular girl's doing commercials now, we've seen her on television, my wife recognized her holding a garden hose in some chemical thing. Her hair's different, all they have to do is cut it off and let it grow back normally, and she's got her breasts under control. So working this market hasn't done her career any harm. We keep a firm eye on the competition, we have to, but there are choices to make. There's a line we won't cross no matter what the competition's doing. And you can make a living without crossing the line.

HARVEY is fifty-six and has worked most of his life at a small factory which makes artificial turf. He has just enough authority at the plant to give him a feeling of satisfaction, and his retirement looks not half bad thanks to some high-interest rates in the eighties. He's been married to the same woman for twenty-four years, and although he's been a little rough with her a few times he's never meant to, it was only because he was real tired and she wouldn't stop and nothing else would work. And she gives as good as she gets. They've got four kids who are going to do all right. Harvey is a sucker for ceremony. His favourite times of the year are Christmas and Thanksgiving when everyone in the family dresses up, sits down and waits for him to carve the turkey. He always wears his suit jacket to the table but halfway through the meal he takes it off and drapes it over the back of his chair. It's a family joke. He's had no major problems over the years, except once in a while with money, but that was not a big surprise.

He found the magazine during a routine drug check through his seventeen-year-old son's dresser. The kid's no trouble and Harvey wants it to stay that way, so he does an inventory once or twice a month. He dug the magazine out of the bottom drawer and flipped through the pages and stopped at our picture.

HARVEY's response: I'll break his ass. If he thinks his mother and I have worked our butts off all these years to have our home polluted with shit like this, he hasn't been paying attention. This would kill his mother. What's wrong with the talent at his school, for God's sake. They better start putting out before he finds himself thinking black and blue is pretty.

RICHARD is Harvey's son, the one with the dresser. He's a fair student and no trouble to anyone. He plays soccer every chance he gets. In his Dad's day it was hockey, but hockey's mostly for the biggest and the baddest now, and Richard's never had the weight. When he was very small his Dad laid a couple of good ones on his rear end to establish the ground rules but he's never touched him since. Richard makes damn sure he has no reason to. He's dark skinned like his mother and he has most of her facial features, including the overbite which has never been attended to, although she dreamed when he was small of getting that done for him. Still, he turns heads. He hangs out with one girl, the first one to say yes to his awkward interest. They eat together at the mall a lot of the time, chinese, tacos, pizza, hamburgers, and they see most of the movies.

She's a big fan of Arnold Schwarzenegger. She thinks he's a riot. And she watches Richard play soccer, although she's not athletic herself. She's not as flashy as some of the others at school, no leather, no nail polish, no hair spray, no boots, no earrings down to her elbows, but she's considerably smarter. She never talks to him much and she just fumbles around if a teacher asks her anything, but she pulls in the A's every time. She came to the house only once, his mother's idea, and she won't come back. When Richard asked her why, she told him the truth, because she thought it was important. She said, guessing he'd likely drop her, "Your Dad makes me sort of uncomfortable." Richard feels her up a lot but she's got control. He thinks she's afraid to touch him.

He bought the magazine for fun, for laughs.

RICHARD's response: Right. So what. That picture's nothing compared to most of it. I can read between the lines.

I know what's normal. I know what the bull means and I know what the chains mean and I know I'm not gonna treat my wife like that. I just like long legs. And I like my privacy. Besides, you start looking for rules about that kind of stuff, you've got to decide who gets to make the rules. And it won't be you and it won't be me. It'll be some loser with a Bible.

JOHN is thirty-four. He sells cameras at a department store. He graduated from university with a fairly good history degree but the system's all plugged up with old teachers, there won't be any jobs, not any time soon, so he signed up for night classes in engineering at the local university. He takes a holiday once a year in the Caribbean with his wife, who is a legal steno with the biggest law firm in the city. They're lucky, their two young children can stay with his mother during the day while they earn the money. He's only ever been in trouble once in his life. When he was in second year at McGill a guy came on to him in the washroom of a pub. He and a friend pounded the guy to a pulp, a reflex action more or less, and subsequently spent the night in jail. But the guy didn't lay any charges. John believed then and he believes now that everyone should get a shot at whatever it is they want, as long as his own path stays clear. His wife's still got most of what she brought to the marriage; she works out and doesn't eat very much. One of the joys of his marriage is seeing heads turn when he meets her at a restaurant downtown for lunch, or when they line up for a movie. He loves taking her south.

He has a subscription to the magazine.

JOHN's response: That's not one of my favourite pictures by any means. The bull and the chains, that stuff will pass. The bull is all souped up on something anyway, guaranteed. Probably more likely to fall over than take off. It's almost an aesthetic thing with me, you know? Women are beautiful and nothing's going to change that. And who would want to change it? My wife doesn't mind, but then she's confident, which she's got every right to be. Nobody's gettin' hurt here.

FATHER MICHAEL is a semi-retired priest who has worked and taught for most of his life in a small Manitoba town. He had been a gentle, shy boy but he gradually learned, with training, how to reach out to people. He looks harmless and has not once in his life raised his voice in anger. He has thanked God for the small successes he has had with the members of his parish. What he's learned is that people, men and women both, usually just need to talk one-to-one with someone who will let them talk.

He found the photograph taped to the wall inside the confessional. He imagines it was put there by the boys. Not one boy, but a group of boys, one who had the idea, one who taped the picture up, and a few others huddled outside the confessional in the spirit of encouragement. He realizes he'll never know who exactly was involved, and this bothers him. It's the secrecy.

FATHER MICHAEL's response: I've been a teacher you should remember. Very little surprises me. I suppose that's why the boys placed the picture there, because they feel the need to surprise me, or to shock me. Children want reaction. They need it sometimes. Defiance is just another word for growing up, isn't it? Perhaps I should make a big show of anger. I've given it some thought. Of course, they have defiled their church and one day down the road some other priest in some other church will hear their confessions. I have prayed for them, they know enough to expect that. As for the woman, as for the photographer and the magazine from which the picture was ripped, that's a bigger prayer, isn't it?

DON is forty. He works as a broker at the Vancouver stock exchange and wears twelve-hundred-dollar suits. He drives a yellow Mercedes 450 SL. He takes his three children regularly and has taught them to sail and to play tennis. He is seeing two women, the social worker regularly and formally and the university student intermittently. He plans to marry again, the social worker, in about two years. He is adept at making people feel good about themselves. His philosophy is that everyone has something going for them. His assistant, whom he hired himself, works out of her house because she's partially paralyzed and uses a wheelchair. She's a crack typist and one of the most precise thinkers he has ever come across. Before his divorce he suffered, briefly, from a kind of impotence, which he regarded as simply an outward manifestation.

He picks up a men's magazine only occasionally, usually because things are a little too tame in his own bed.

DON's response: It's been going on from the beginning of time. And fifty years from now, count on it, we'll be back to modesty, prudery. That's where we're headed. Some day soon the mere glimpse of a woman's ankle will drive a man mad again. It's like lapels. Narrow, wide, narrow, wide. But right now this threshold is the one we're on and this is where the thrills are. Take it or leave it. Nobody's forcing anything. The bruises are make-up, the bull is doped, and the farmer will have something to remember, likely bought his wife a dishwasher with the money the bull earned. The young lady knows what she's doin' and a lot of people would probably thank her for it. Maybe you've noticed that hookers are fighting in court for the right to hook. And I read in *Harper's* about a prostitute, a free woman in a free country, who will let men spit on her for a quick twenty bucks. What's it to you and me? There are bigger problems. Read the paper, any paper.

DR. FRANCIS ELMERS is an obstetrician. He is fifty. His wife is a dentist. They have a daughter who is just finishing her first degree; she's a sensible, serious kid. She's got an academic record which will allow her to choose from almost anything the world has to offer. For twelve years Dr. Elmers has rented an acre of land at the sunny nonindustrial edge of the city. Each year he plants a garden there and he retreats to this garden when he is overtired. He is extremely good looking and even at fifty is still dealing with the inevitable infatuation of some of his undeniably beautiful pregnant patients. In spite of his long-term professional attendance at open birth canals and at the surgical incisions made necessary by C-Sections, in spite of his familiarity with blood and pain and complications, Dr. Elmers regards birth and all things which make it possible, particularly the bodies of women, as miracles. He has never lost either a mother or a baby in childbirth, although there have been failures, deformities, physiological aberrations that would shock outsiders. In these cases, almost always, nature takes its course.

He has consistently refused to sit on the abortion panel at the hospital where he has privileges and, although his daughter occasionally accuses him of hiding his head in the sand, he remains firm. He believes in full state support for young women who must raise their babies alone, and he believes this support should be collected by the state from the young men whose sperm seems recently to be so profuse. He has defended these opinions at many dinner parties. When he was in medical school, his girlfriend, a nursing student, became pregnant.

They couldn't marry and she gave the child up. In moments of weakness he catches himself wishing she'd kept the child because he sees now, in retrospect, that he would have been able to contribute financially without much strain. But usually he takes the attitude, what's done is done. Another of his secrets is that he has been a long-time collector of erotica, not actual photographs or books but carefully selected images to hold in his mind.

Dr. Elmers saw the magazine at counter level in a narrow little convenience store near the hospital, where he'd stopped to buy breath mints. He lifted it out and leafed through it quickly. When he saw the bull he asked to see the store manager. He told the manager to get this material behind the counter or he'd have himself a visit he wouldn't forget.

DR. ELMERS's response: Beneath contempt. It is not worth serious discussion.

RAYMOND is twenty-two. He has almost finished serving a reduced four years of an eight-year sentence in Kingston for break and enter with a weapon. He's tall, he's got a good muscular build from working out and his face, which is almost a ringer for River Phoenix's face, is still softly scored with the scars of adolescent acne. He grew up in the East, in poverty, in a family where nurturing meant there was nearly enough to eat. He doesn't even think his father's name but he writes to his mother and to his youngest sister every week, she's had a baby whose middle name is Raymond. Prison has given him the chance to get his grade twelve and he's also taken some mechanics training; they say he's a natural. He feels pretty sure there'll be a job waiting when he gets out, which will be soon. He knows it was a major error getting involved with the guys who organized the thing. He was just young and stupid. He was only taking a few months to knock around before he signed on with the mine. He's no criminal. They gave him the gun and he held it all right, but to this day he doesn't know how to fire one. Although he'd never share that. He keeps his nose firmly out of other people's business and his mouth shut, a skill which he figures is a whole hell of a lot more valuable than knowing how to use a gun. There are lots of knives and drugs around, but not as many as people think, it's not compulsory. He has been approached a few times in the showers, and once, early on, he didn't get away, but there was just that once, before he started to work out. New guys will sometimes select him and try to buddy him up, looking for protection from the unknown. But it's not available, at least not from him.

A friend threw the magazine at him in the prison library.

RAYMOND's response: I'll tell you how it makes me feel. I'd be delighted. You want all the slimy details? You have time? I'll tell you what they got here to offer the average man is sweet nothin'. There is nothing soft or easy in this place. So we *respond* to pictures. You want to hear about the alternatives? You think we're the guys who hurt women? You're wrong. The last thing I wanna do to a woman when I'm outta here is hurt her. There'll be a woman all right, maybe several dozen, but they won't be gettin' hurt and they sure as hell won't look like this one. A bull, for God's sake. What's that, a stockbroker's wet dream?

RYAN is five years old, and of course he doesn't quite qualify as a man. But he'll get there, faster than he thinks. He lives in an apartment in a decent neighbourhood with his single mother, who receives fair and adequate maintenance payments from his father, who doesn't believe in marriage. She has explained their circumstances to Ryan, using language he can understand, trying to protect his feelings about his usually absent father. She is a thoughtful and careful woman, in every respect. She didn't automatically enrol Ryan in the closest nursery school but first interviewed several teachers in several different schools around the city. Ryan eats every vegetable but cauliflower and brussels sprouts, he can read a bit, he runs hard and flat out whenever he gets the chance, and he considers himself an accomplished kid. His mother has instilled that confidence in him because she considers it his birthright. She wants them to have their own separate house, away from the stink of the apartment halls and the dingy laundry room and the passing of strangers on the stairs. She inherited twenty thousand dollars for a down payment from her father, who died of an aneurysm in the spring, and she thinks she could manage a small house if she works full-time when Ryan goes to school.

She had to leave Ryan with a neighbour friend when she went downtown for a job interview. Ryan and Cody, the neighbour's boy, found the magazine in a bathroom drawer. Cody took it out of the drawer but it slipped from his hands and dropped to the tile floor, fell open to our photograph. They stared down at the woman and the bull for a few seconds, they saw the pubic hair and the bruises and the thick tongue hanging from the bull's mouth, and then Cody jumped on the page, jumped up and down on it and laughed, as little boys do. Neither of them had seen a naked woman before, they couldn't even remember their mothers' breasts, although they'd both been nursed as infants. Caught, they said they were just looking for some more toilet paper.

RYAN's response: When his mother asks him about the magazine, in her careful, thoughtful way, he says nothing, except that he's sorry and that he will never go looking through other people's things again, which is a lie for which he might be excused. She tells him it's okay and the only really important thing he has to remember is that magazines like that have nothing to do with them. He listens, he hears what she says, but he knows he's discovered something, something no one would have told him about if he hadn't found it for himself. Like the snakes that crawl around in the woodpile at the farm, for the shade, his uncle said. Or the slugs he found under the tomato leaves in his other grandmother's garden, trailing what she called mucus but he calls something else. Or the dark round thing that grows under his mother's arm, a mole, she said, it's only an ordinary mole, which he saw by mistake the very last time he charged into her room without knocking.

ACKNOWLEDGMENTS

I am grateful to the following publications in which some of these stories appeared in an earlier form: "Crush" in *NeWest Review* (1984), *Double Bond* (1984), *Worlds Unrealized* (1991), *Kitchen Talk: Contemporary Women's Prose and Poetry* (1992); "Patsy Flater's Brief Search for God" in *Grain* (1992), *Lodestone: Stories by Regina Writers*; "Casino" in *Best Canadian Stories* (1992); "Deer Heart" in *Best Canadian Stories* (1989), *Soho Square III* (1990), *Kunapipi* (1991); "Figurines" in *Beyond Borders* (1992).

"Casino" also aired on "Ambience" (CBC Regina).

The author would like to thank the Saskatchewan Arts Board and the Canada Council for their support of this manuscript.

ABOUT THE AUTHOR

Bonnie Burnard is a writer, editor and reviewer whose work
has been widely anthologized and dramatized on the CBC.
She won the Commonwealth Best First Book Award for
Women of Influence and has also won several Saskatchewan
Writers' Guild Awards. She was the fiction editor for *Grain*
magazine from 1982 to 1986 and has given readings through-
out Canada, the U.S.A., England, Europe, South Africa and
Australia. Bonnie Burnard lives in Ontario.

📖 HarperCollins*CanadaLtd*

Are there any HarperCollins books you want but cannot find in your local bookstore?

If so, you can probably special order them from your local bookstore. Ask at the cash desk or customer service desk for more information about <u>special ordering</u>, a service available at better bookstores across Canada. Your local bookseller will be happy to be of assistance.